ARIS & PHILLIPS HISPANIC CLASSICS

T0341350

RAMÓN DEL VALLE-INCLÁN

The Dead Man's Finery

Las galas del difunto

and

The Captain's Daughter

La hija del capitán

Translation, Introduction and Notes by
Laura Lonsdale

Aris & Phillips
is an imprint of
Oxbow Books, Oxford, UK

ISBN   hardback: 978-1-90834-325-3
ISBN   paper: 978-1-90834-324-6

A CIP record for this book is available from the British Library.

This book is available direct from

Oxbow Books, Oxford, UK
Phone: 01865-241249; Fax: 01865-794449

and

The David Brown Book Company
PO Box 511, Oakville, CT 06779, USA
Phone: 860-945-9329; Fax: 860-945-9468

or from our website

www.oxbowbooks.com

*Cover image: ©Photo SCALA, Florence. Grosz, George (1893–1959): Gray Day. 1921.
Berlin, Nationalgalerie, Staatliche Museen zu Berlin. Oil on canvas, 115.0 × 80.0 cm.
Inv. B97. Photo: Joerg P. Anders.© 2012. Photo Scala, Florence/BPK, Bildagentur fuer
Kunst, Kultur und Geschichte, Berlin*

Printed and bound by CPI Group (UK) Ltd, Croydon, CR0 4YY

CONTENTS

TRANSLATOR'S NOTE

Translating Valle-Inclán is an intensely rewarding and equally frustrating task: his language is so elusively and eccentrically innovative that it may be something of a fool's errand even to attempt to translate it. But at the same time his work is so insufficiently known outside the Spanish-speaking world that it seems a shame not to try. Moreover, though it is his use of language that marks out Valle-Inclán as one of the greatest writers in Spanish, the dramatic and visual language of his plays is also highly innovative and imaginative, and deserves to be interpreted more often on an international stage.

Valle-Inclán's Spanish is filled with regionalisms, Americanisms, colloquialisms, archaisms, neologisms, bizarre turns of phrase, and the specialised vocabulary of bullfighting or the military; this can make it very difficult, firstly, to interpret what he means, and secondly, to render the meaning in English without domesticating it too much or producing something hideously contrived. Like so much really excellent writing, Valle-Inclán's texts use language in ways that are surprising and eclectic, so that obscurity is often compensated by the sense of possibility it generates. It is often acknowledged that even Spaniards are foxed by Valle-Inclán's unusual Spanish, as the array of footnotes to critical editions of his works attest. The plays translated in this edition are not as linguistically challenging as some of Valle-Inclán's later prose works, such as *Tirano Banderas [Banderas the Tyrant]* or *La corte de los milagros [The Court of Miracles]*, but the greatest challenge they present is their particular use of the popular idiom. The great talent Valle-Inclán possessed as a writer is evident in, among other things, his ability to make often vulgar language poetic, to attend to rhythm and cadence even in the language of thieves and prostitutes, and to make lexical choices that are always rich and expressive. As Francisco Umbral eloquently puts it in his very insightful study of the author:

> Valle parece que ha inventado el diálogo artístico, como pudiéramos llamarlo, y esto lo han tomado muchos críticos por lujo inútil. Muy al contrario, Valle es el único escritor español, con Quevedo y los barrocos, que ha sabido hacer hablar a la gente, a toda una raza, no mediante la reproducción mecánica del coloquialismo (realismo galdobarojiano), sino

mediante una estilización y síntesis que elevan cualquier localismo a un nivel de significación mayor.

Valle invented what we might call artistic dialogue, which many critics have interpreted as pointlessly self-indulgent. On the contrary, however, Valle is the only Spanish writer, along with Quevedo and the writers of the baroque, who has been able to make people speak, to make a whole race speak, not by mechanically reproducing colloquial language (like the realists Galdós and Baroja), but through a stylisation and synthesis that elevate any localism to a plane of greater significance.

(1998, 150; my translation)

The plays translated here were written during the 1920s but are in no sense linguistic period pieces. This is ultimately liberating for the translator, who is not compelled to recreate a particular dialect or mode of expression, but it does demand a constant seeking out and weaving together of words that can, as it were, clash sonorously and productively.

In an attempt to at least partly emulate the variety of Valle-Inclán's use of language, I have drawn on a number of linguistic sources, of which two of the most significant are John Gay's *The Beggar's Opera* and the genre of hardboiled detective fiction. Though they belong to vastly differing times and places, they are both a rich source of colourful expressions associated with the criminal underworld. *The Beggar's Opera* features a cast of characters with names markedly reminiscent of some of the protagonists of *La hija del capitán/The Captain's Daughter*: Jemmy Twitcher, Crook-Fingered Jack, Suky Tawdry, *etc*. Both sources helped me to overcome the relative impoverishment of a more standard lexicon of obscenities in colloquial expressions of anger, frustration, *etc*., and for vocabulary associated with killing, thieving, prostitution, and so on. Other sources that provided inspiration and variety were the Jumieka Langwij Dikshineri (Jamaican Language Dictionary) and the novels of Andrea Levy, in connection with the Caribbean backdrop to both plays; the novels of P. G. Wodehouse, filled to bursting with the early 20th century English vernacular; the online Urban Dictionary; cockney rhyming slang; and the 'digger' slang of Anzac military forces during the two world wars. This internationalism is intended to reflect Valle-Inclán's own borderless engagement with the Spanish language, and is designed also to add verbal texture to the translations.

My main concern in drawing on such a wide range of linguistic sources was to ensure that the words and expressions I chose didn't belong too recognisably to a particular period, nation, or genre: I didn't want to just stitch together jarring bits of slang from opposite sides of the Atlantic and vastly different time periods. The aim was therefore to choose words that sounded unusual, colloquial and expressive but which would not obviously call to mind mutually contradictory times or places. Words and expressions such as 'lam off' (run away), 'bilker' (cheat), 'blip' (kill), 'shank' (stab), 'diver' (pickpocket), 'grifter/jinal' (con man) seem to me not sufficiently familiar to average speakers of English to make them recall 18th century London, 1930s Chicago, 21st century Jamaica, or a modern prison, yet their expressive potential is evident. The same could be said of 'Wouldn't it rot your socks!' (A 'digger' expression of disgust). Valle-Inclán does not use colloquial language in the name of enhanced realism but to evoke an atmosphere of 'chulería' or coarse vulgarity, an atmosphere which is violent but also humorous.

In spite of the linguistic variety provided by these sources, the idiomatic base of the translation is clearly modern British English, though I have attempted to avoid words or turns of phrase that I consider to be very current: I wanted the colloquial, coarse tone of the language to remain literary and strange, to avoid making it too familiar to the contemporary reader, foreshortening in the process the historical and cultural distance between the reader and the original text. There are some exceptions to this rule, where I judged that the comedic value of a certain expression in a certain situation (such as the Witch and the Callow Youth telling each other to 'Get stuffed') outweighed other considerations. Cockney rhyming slang is useful in maintaining an element of strangeness because it introduces an apparently incongruous word into a sentence without completely obscuring the meaning (*e.g.* 'whistle' for 'suit' (whistle and flute); 'plink-plonk' for 'wine' (vin blanc); 'bits' for 'tits' (threepenny bits)). Again, I've tried to avoid any instances of rhyming slang that have become part of Eastend folklore and so too culturally specific (*e.g.* 'dog and bone' (phone) or 'apples and pears' (stairs)). For utterances that seemed to beg for an expletive I have sometimes used an invented adjective, 'copping,' avoiding expressions that are either more obscene than their Spanish equivalents or, worse still, quaintly old-fashioned. I have used 'Christ' and 'Christ Almighty' on a number of occasions for both their irreverence and sense of urgency.

It is inevitable that much of Valle-Inclán's craft will be lost in the process of translation, but I hope that these bilingual texts will stimulate the curious reader into engaging further with his extraordinary use of language.

Critical Introduction

The Esperpento *and* Martes de carnaval

In 1930, Valle-Inclán brought together three previously published plays in a collection entitled *Martes de Carnaval*. Their common satirical target was the culture of the Spanish military, which for Valle-Inclán encapsulated the worst and most retrogressive values of Spanish society. The title of the collection refers to Shrove Tuesday or Mardi Gras, the culmination of the traditional period of carnival and feasting before the beginning of the Lenten fast, a period normally marked by public festivities which had been banned in Madrid under Primo de Rivera's military dictatorship (1923–1930). Creating a pun on the word Martes (Tuesday/Mars), Valle-Inclán uses this date in the Christian calendar to ironically evoke the god of war in the context of a carnival masquerade. By rendering his military characters and their situations grotesque and absurd, the distorted puppet figures of the plays become 'martes de carnaval,' or carnivalesque gods of war.

The three plays included in the collection were *Las galas del difunto/ The Dead Man's Finery, Esperpento de los cuernos de Don Friolera/The Grotesque Farce of Mr Punch the Cuckold*, and *La hija del capitán/The Captain's Daughter*, the first and last of which are translated here for the first time into English. They were conceived within the framework of Valle-Inclán's recently defined genre of the *esperpento*, a genre that combines puppetry and farce with bitter satire. The first example of this new genre was *Luces de Bohemia/Lights of Bohemia*, generally regarded as Valle's theatrical masterpiece, published first in 1920 and again in a significantly revised version in 1924. Exploiting the word's various associations with ugliness, extravagance, and bad theatre, the *esperpento* was Valle-Inclán's aesthetic response to the 'deformación grotesca de la civilización europea' [grotesque deformation of European civilization] that he considered Spain to have become (*Luces* 169).[1] The sheer absurdity, as he saw it, of the times in which he was living led Valle-Inclán to explore new and daring ways of expressing Spanish reality,

---

[1]   All translations are mine unless otherwise indicated.

the culmination of which was the creation of the *esperpento*. In the four plays he classified within this new genre, Valle-Inclán attacked Spain's institutions for their self-interest, hypocrisy and moral bankruptcy. He depicted the government, the army, and the monarchy at the sharp end of a society mired in superstition and bad literature, anachronistically vaunting Spain's glorious past and yet steeped in a contemporary pettiness. He portrayed a pragmatic society motivated by materialism and a rapacious instinct for self-preservation, in which love, politics and religion were reduced to cliché and insincere bluster.

The army was a particular target for Valle-Inclán both because of the role it had played historically in Spanish political life, and because of the pronounced disjunction between its protestations of military honour on the one hand and its humiliating failures on the international stage on the other, particularly its defeat in the Spanish-American War of 1898. Most recently, a disastrous defeat and massacre of Spanish troops in Morocco in 1921 at the battle of Annual had led to the royally-approved proclamation of Primo de Rivera's military dictatorship, amid rumours of incompetence and corruption which implicated even the King. When the writer and philosopher Miguel de Unamuno, then Rector of the Universidad de Salamanca, was exiled to the Canary Islands in 1924 for his vociferous opposition to the regime, Valle-Inclán responded with an open condemnation of both the King and the dictator, whom he irreverently and respectively dubbed 'el beodo' [the drunk] and 'el cretino' [the cretin] (Lima 2003, 147). He further branded the King a 'muñeco grotesco' [grotesque puppet] (Lima 2003, 147), and indeed Valle's writing of the 1920s is full of grotesque puppets acting out a mechanical and self-interested hypocrisy. The military theme that unifies *Martes de carnaval* undoubtedly emerged in response to these events, but it was enhanced with a view to creating greater thematic cohesion between the plays (Senabre 1990, 21). In *Las galas/Finery*, for example, Valle-Inclán introduced a number of direct and damning references to the war in Cuba which were absent from the play's first incarnation as *El terno del difunto/The Dead Man's Suit* (1926). He made similar revisions to *Don Friolera/Mr Punch* (1921) to emphasise army corruption, and he changed the location of *Capitán/Captain* (1927) from the fictional Tartarinesia to the very real setting of Madrid. In this way, Valle-Inclán linked three separately conceived plays to generate a series with clear thematic and structural cohesion, organised both by chronology and rank: *Las galas/Finery* is set in 1898 and features a squaddie; *Don Friolera/Mr Punch* appears to take place around the time of the Moroccan campaign of 1921 and portrays a lieutenant; *Capitán/Captain* clearly satirises Primo de Rivera's 1923 coup and points the finger at some of Spain's most high-ranking military officers. This organisation explains why *Don Friolera/Mr Punch* is sandwiched between the two shorter plays, in spite of the fact that it was written first (Cardona and Zahareas 1970, 187, 213).

Valle-Inclán's primary intention in creating the *esperpento* was therefore to formulate an appropriate literary response to contemporary reality, which in his view had degenerated into a grotesque farce. The satirical vision of social and political reality is framed, in at least three of the four *esperpentos*, by a response to a range of past and present literary modes as well as by historical events. Disgusted by the bourgeois sentimentality and lack of innovation that characterised the commercial theatre of his day, Valle-Inclán sought to develop a new aesthetic vision, a new dramatic mode that would reflect the national problem as he saw it, replacing the mirror of Realism with the convex mirror of a fairground or the bottom of a drunkard's glass. In the process he parodied a range of high- and low-brow literary forms, including the Calderonian honour play, the sensationalist *romance de ciegos* [blind men's ballad],[2] the Don Juan myth, and the nineteenth century *folletín* or melodrama. Challenging both the tragic-heroic vision, including its most vulgar manifestations, and the psychological detail of naturalism, Valle-Inclán displaced the theatrical hero with anti-naturalistic figures in the grip of their own puppet farce. In this way, Valle-Inclán applied his complex artistic vision to the present and to the recent past in a way he had refused to do before the *esperpento*, extending the range of his experimental dramatic language in order to tackle contemporary themes.

Valle-Inclán theorised his new genre, first described as the 'género

---

[2] 'One of the commonest modes of popular diffusion of the ballad up until the nineteenth century [...] was the *romance de ciegos* (blind men's ballad). The blind man was not only a performer but also a seller of ballads [...] Such figures were a common sight especially in the south of Spain and were converted into a literary type or commonplace. Although varied in content [these *romances* were characterised by] their tendency to over-statement through the exaggeration of emotion and the quest for the lurid detail [...]' (Walters 2002, 87).

estrafalario' or 'extravagant genre', in the first two plays he classified within it: *Luces de Bohemia/Lights of Bohemia* (1920/24) and *Los cuernos de Don Friolera/Mr Punch the Cuckold* (1921). Both these plays establish the *esperpento* as a distortion of tragedy, highlighting the incongruity of the tragic idiom in the context of contemporary Spanish reality. As the protagonist of *Luces/Lights*, Max Estrella, famously explains:

> Los héroes clásicos reflejados en los espejos cóncavos dan el Esperpento. El sentido trágico de la vida española sólo puede darse con una estética sistemáticamente deformada.

> The *Esperpento* is born when classical heroes are reflected in concave mirrors. The only artistic vision that can express the tragic sense of Spanish life is one that systematically deforms what it sees.
>
> (*Luces* 168–69)

For Valle, Spain's contemporary reality was not a tragedy but a farcical distortion of tragedy. This notion of the *esperpento* as the reflection of a society incapable of dignity or heroism was one that Valle-Inclán consistently emphasised:

> Ustedes saben que en las tragedias antiguas, los personajes marchaban al destino trágico, valiéndose del gesto trágico. Yo en mi nuevo género también conduzco a los personajes al destino trágico, pero me valgo para ello del gesto ridículo. En la vida existen muchos seres que llevan la tragedia dentro de sí y que son incapaces de una actitud levantada, resultando, por el contrario, grotescos en todos sus actos.
>   Esta modalidad – se refiere al esperpento – consiste en buscar el lado cómico en lo trágico de la vida misma.

> As you all know, in ancient tragedy characters marched towards their tragic destiny in a tragic manner. In my new genre I also drive my characters towards a tragic destiny, but they approach it in a ridiculous manner. There are many people in life with the potential to be tragic, but because they haven't the capacity to be dignified, they become grotesque in everything they do.
>   This mode – I'm referring now to the *esperpento* – consists in seeking comedy in the tragedy of life itself.
>
> (Quoted in J. del Valle-Inclán 2007, 252)

The artistic vision of the *esperpento* was one that Valle-Inclán attributed primarily to the painter Francisco de Goya, though he also associated it with the 17th century satirist Francisco de Quevedo and with Cervantes's *Don Quixote*. Goya's etchings of war and the paintings of his *época negra* [black period] are both emotionally intense and yet completely lacking in grandeur or sentimentality, conveying emotional detachment but also great emotional power. The significance of this artistic perspective is highlighted in *Friolera/Mr Punch*. The play begins with a prologue in which two men, Don Manolito and Don Estrafalario, are discussing a painting. Don Manolito considers that an artwork is good if it is realistic and succeeds in provoking an emotional response in the viewer:

> Hay que amar, Don Estrafalario: la risa y las lágrimas son los caminos de Dios. Ésa es mi estética y la de usted.

> Love above all things, Don Estrafalario: laughter and tears will bring us to God. That is my artistic philosophy, and yours too.

> *(Martes* 124)

Don Estrafalario, however, makes the case for a very different kind of art:

> Mi estética es una superación del dolor y de la risa, como deben ser las conversaciones de los muertos, al contarse historias de los vivos […] Yo quisiera ver este mundo con la perspectiva de la otra ribera.

> In my artistic philosophy laughter and pain are overcome. Imagine a conversation between the dead, as they tell each other stories about the living […] I would like to view this world as if I were on the opposite side of the river.

> *(Martes* 124)

A sentimental reaction, as Don Estrafalario sees it, is the product of a messy identification between oneself and another living being. His ideal perspective is therefore that of the 'otra ribera,' the opposite side of the mythological river Styx: from this position he can be completely separate from all living beings, and can regard them with ironic detachment. For Don Estrafalario, the truly aesthetic perspective is a detached one: the sentimental spectator moved to tears by the plight of a horse at a bullfight is incapable of appreciating the 'emoción estética' [aesthetic emotion] of the fight. He dismissively concludes that the sensibility of such a spectator is essentially equine. Valle distinguishes in this way between sentiment and emotion: Goya is full of emotion, but lacks sentiment; the same can be said of the bullfight. In 1925, the philosopher José Ortega y Gasset famously wrote that modern art was 'dehumanised' art, by which he meant that it did not exist merely to provoke 'human' (read sentimental) reactions in the viewer or reader. Like Don Estrafalario, Ortega also identified Don Manolito's realistic and sentimental kind of art with a lack of aesthetic sensibility. In fact the whole movement of art in the 1920s was towards this more 'dehumanised' perspective, which Valle interpreted in his own particular way through the *esperpento*.

The esperpentic vision that Valle theorised in *Luces/Lights* and *Friolera/Mr Punch* is evident throughout both the plays in this edition. Though they don't contain the theoretical ballast of the other *esperpentos*, they nevertheless contribute significantly to a definition of the genre. As John Lyon observes, there is a clear evolution or at least a considerable degree of variation in Valle-Inclán's employment of the genre (1983, 106), and the two shorter plays of *Martes de carnaval* are essential to a proper understanding of it.

Las galas del difunto/The Dead Man's Finery

El terno del difunto/The Dead Man's Suit appeared in Madrid-based literary journal *La Novela Mundial* in 1926, at the height of Primo de Rivera's dictatorship. Its author first described it as a novel, refusing as he often did to distinguish between the novel in dialogue and the play, claiming that his works were written to be read rather than performed. As Ricardo Senabre notes, the play has perhaps as much in common with such macabre farces as *La rosa de papel* [*The Paper Rose*] and *La cabeza del Bautista* [*The Baptist's Head*] as it does with the *esperpentos* (1990, 20), but Valle-Inclán chose to emphasise the play's setting at the end of the Spanish-American war in order to incorporate it into a collection of works satirising the military 'family.'

Las galas del difunto/The Dead Man's Finery is a short dramatic incursion into the life of Juanito Ventolera/Johnny Bluster, a decommissioned veteran of the Spanish-American War who steals a dead man's clothes in order to woo a prostitute. A recreation of the Don Juan legend, the play to some extent parodies José Zorrilla's Romantic version of the myth, in which the devilish Don Juan is transformed into a figure redeemed by the love of a pure woman. This is a consistent source of bathos in Valle-Inclán's play, in which the rapturous purity of feeling that passes between Don Juan and Doña Inés is replaced with jocular dialogue filled with sexual innuendo. This deflating technique is enhanced by a recourse to cliché, and by frequent changes of register that point to the characters' tendency to express themselves in received ways. Though a concern with belittling mythical archetypes remains, Valle-Inclán does not satisfy himself in this play with undermining a hero by portraying him as a puppet. Rather, he takes the already problematic, protean and devilish Don Juan and sets his outrageous behaviour in a very particular social and historical context.

John Lyon argues that *Las galas/Finery* and *Capitán/Captain* display a marked evolution in Valle-Inclán's conception of the *esperpento*. Whereas *Luces/Lights* presents us with a potential hero reduced to a pathetic figure by his surroundings, and *Friolera/Mr Punch* depicts a manipulated puppet incapable of thinking outside institutionalised codes, the shorter plays are peopled with characters no better and no worse than the society around them. In this way, the individual disappears from view and a more social protagonist emerges (1983, 150). An emphasis on the inadequate hero does remain in the Don Juan figure of *Las galas/Finery*, and in the vain proclamations of the crapulous General in *Capitán/Captain*; but whereas Max and Friolera are embryonic heroes that singularly fail to live up to their tragic potential, the characters of the shorter plays lack any such potential. In other words, the tragic frame within which the *esperpento* is initially conceived is no longer present in the shorter plays: in *Las galas/Finery* it has been replaced with the dramatic and mythical frame of Don Juan, whilst *Capitán/Captain* has dispensed with sustained literary allusion altogether. The two later plays are not only shorter than the earlier ones but are also divided into seven scenes with a highly organised structure. This delight in patterns is nowhere more evident than in the novel that Valle-Inclán wrote around the same time as these later *esperpentos, Tirano Banderas*, which is itself carefully structured around the magical numbers three and seven.

Whilst both *Friolera/Mr Punch* and *Capitán/Captain* make it almost impossible for us to identify or sympathise with any of the characters, from whom we are consistently and systematically alienated, *Las galas/ Finery* does not dehumanise its protagonists so completely. Like the characters of *Friolera/Mr Punch* they are circumscribed by cliché, but this produces a different order of mechanical behaviour. The honour code to which Don Friolera adheres is so manifestly at odds both with morality and justice that his eventual acceptance of it confirms his behaviour as absurdly automatic. The codes that regulate the behaviour of Juanito Ventolera/Johnny Bluster and the Daifa/Courtesan are much more subtle, however, and as characters they are barely conscious of them. Furthermore, the environment that structures Friolera's behaviour is corrupt and ludicrous, and Friolera is vulnerable to it because he is foolish and weak. Juanito/Johnny, on the other hand, a soldier returning from the Spanish-American war in Cuba, is vulnerable to his environment in quite a different way.

The historical significance of the Cuban War of Independence and subsequent Spanish-American war cannot be overstated, given that the loss of Spain's last overseas colonies in 1898 gave rise to a profound sense of humiliation and national inferiority. As historian Rafael Núñez Florencio explains:

> It would have been possible to describe a situation "more appropriate to comedy", if it hadn't been for the high price the nation paid in blood, for all the errors and the ineptitude, and above all, from a historical point of view, for the pathetic role that Spain played on the international stage. So we return to drama, [...] but not to tragedy. Neither the vision nor the effort was grand enough for that. There was no epic encounter for the Spanish army, no Waterloo that could be justified in terms of material inferiority. Not even the laments of the intellectuals that came after the war can be dissociated from this sense that Spain had made a fool of itself. Sadly Spain had not fallen with dignity. It had been... something else.
>
> (1999, 34)

In keeping with such an interpretation, Valle-Inclán strips the historical events of 1898 of any glory or transcendence, reducing the war to an ignominious skirmish conducted by pompous Generals, whose conscripts are left destitute on their return to the mother country. Juanito's extraordinary and sacrilegious behaviour – his robbing of the grave for a suit of new clothes – is therefore his response to the dumb show of a war without glory. He may be reduced to a blustering, arrogant drunkard desperate for a seedy bourgeois respectability, but when the play begins he is both lucidly critical and physically vulnerable, not unlike the blind Max Estrella in *Luces/Lights*.

The return of demobilized soldiers from the colonial wars was a highly emotive issue in the years immediately before and after 1898. The first accounts of the precarious health of the soldiers returning to the peninsula date from 1896, when 'returning soldiers began to be depicted as terminally ill individuals, consumed by yellow fever, ghostly figures dressed in rags, barefoot, skeletal men shivering beneath threadbare blankets; in short, as living corpses. All these descriptions […] later were repeated *ad nauseam* to the point of cliché […]' (Núñez 1999, 35). The description of Juanito/Johnny and the other 'febrile' soldiers in their striped uniforms very much conforms to this stereotype:

> Alto, flaco, macilento, los ojos de fiebre, la manta terciada, el gorro en la oreja, la trasquila en la sien. El tinglado de cruces y medallas daba sus brillos buhoneros.

> Tall, thin and wan, his eyes febrile, his cloak lopsided, his cap tilted to one side, his head shorn above the temples. The jumble of crosses and medals glitters on his uniform like a pedlar's wares.

> (pp. 44–5)

Expected to behave like a hero though he hasn't a penny to his name, on his return to Spain Juanito/Johnny is forced to choose between action and resignation, and he chooses the former. His sacrilegious act of defiance is therefore a product of a very specific set of historical and institutional circumstances, which may not justify his actions but which nevertheless gives them a flavour of existential assertiveness. This is entirely lacking in Max, who is incapable of action, and in Friolera, who is vacillating, weak, and always at the mercy of the judgements of others. Friolera's attempt to punish his wayward wife is therefore a ludicrous and senseless gesture of conformity. In the same way, Friolera is a victim of rhetoric, whilst Juanito/Johnny is a manipulator of language, his register fluid, his tone ironic: this anoints him with the satanic attractiveness that Don Juan has always exploited as a character. The appeal that immoral characters can hold for readers is something that has tended to trouble moralists, but Valle-Inclán was never truly a moralist: he was instead a dramatist who pushed moral and emotional situations to their limit, provoking in his spectator an agonising combination of laughter, horror, pain, sympathy and revulsion. This was true even in much earlier works such as the early *Comedias bárbaras [Barbaric Comedies]* in which the aristocratic protagonist is both violent abuser and messianic patriarch. But whereas the historical context of the *Comedias bárbaras* remains mythical and vague, in *Las galas/Finery* history comes acutely and prominently to the fore. In Juanito Ventolera/Johnny Bluster, Valle-Inclán presents us with a character whose terrible actions are the product of a shameful national situation, which includes not only the lost war and bungled repatriation of soldiers, but also the petty hypocrisy of the bourgeois society to which the soldiers return. It is this society, represented by the chemist, the barber and the sexton, to which Juanito/Johnny seeks access through the symbolic donning of a new suit of clothes. His actions are therefore unworthy and grotesque, but they are not risible, nor are they especially mechanical. Considered alongside other protagonists of the *esperpento*, he offers a different manifestation of the absurd: he is not the ailing and impotent visionary that we have in Max Estrella, nor is he a manipulated puppet like Friolera. The cynicism he shares with Don Latino and La Sini is to some extent offset by his circumstances. Though he is a soldier, his bitterness towards the army chiefs prevents him from being representative of corrupt military values. Valle-Inclán is a long way from endorsing Juanito's actions, but in the character's desire to stand proud against the whole world 'with the devil for company' (p. 69) is encapsulated a profoundly modern and existential form of absurdity. Valle-Inclán was not the only author to see this potential in the Don Juan legend, though it is perhaps by regarding the play as a new version of the legend rather than just a parody of it that Valle-Inclán's exploitation of this potential becomes evident.

However, it should be remembered that Valle-Inclán was writing this play long after the events of 1898, when the image of the 'living corpses' returning from the war must already have turned to cliché in the public imagination. Aside from the fact that a 'living corpse' fits nicely into Valle's theatrical repertory of dead bodies and the play's graveyard motif, it is likely that Valle chose this image of the returning soldier not only for its capacity to encapsulate a very specific historical moment, but also for its relative lack of novelty. This lack of novelty must surely have extended to the historical moment itself and even to the anguished intellectual response it provoked: whilst 1898 had defined a whole generation of writers and thinkers in Spain, their concerns and modes of expression had become outdated by the mid-1920s. For all that Juanito is potentially humanised by his vulnerability at the start of the play, this is tempered by the fact that he is already a cliché, perhaps even a caricature.

The parodic references to Zorrilla's *Don Juan Tenorio* are also significant in this context, as they provide a repertoire of visual and linguistic references that an average Spaniard would have been easily able to identify. J. B. Avalle-Arce tells us that Zorrilla's play belonged firmly to the literary culture of the masses, becoming 'semi-esperpentizado' [practically an *esperpento* in its own right] on its journey through the popular tradition (1959, 35). Even in the 1960s Oscar Mandel asserted that 'every Spanish schoolboy can recite Zorrilla' (1963, 468) The popularity of the *Don Juan Tenorio* no doubt owed itself in part to the fact that the Romantic poet and dramatist's version of the legend is, as Mandel puts it, 'full of the melodrama, the cheap spiritual flights, the sentimentalities, and the scenic crowding that all but killed the theatre in the nineteenth century. It is opera more than play' (1963, 467). Valle-Inclán no doubt admired the operatic qualities of the play (he certainly admired Zorrilla), but its sentimental populism was also grist to the artistic mill of the *esperpento*. If we bring together the employment of timeworn topoi of the events of 1898, the association between Juanito/Johnny and a populist Don Juan, and Juanito's assumption of the cloak of bourgeois respectability, we have a character whose identity is stitched together out of well-worn cultural guises.

The story of the Coima/Courtesan's plight, like Juanito's story, also has the power to humanise and inspire empathy:

> Todos [los soldados] volvéis con la misma polca, pero ello es que os llevan y os traen como borregos. Y si fueseis solos a pasar las penalidades, os estaría muy bien puesto. Pero las consecuencias alcanzan a los más inocentes, y un hijo que hoy estaría criándose a mi lado, lo tengo en la Maternidad. Esta vida en que me ves, se la debo a esa maldita guerra que no sabéis acabar [...] Se fue dejándome embarazada de cinco meses. Pasado un poco más tiempo no pude tenerlo oculto, y al descubrirse, mi padre me echó al camino. Por donde también a mí me alcanza la guerra.

> You [soldiers] all come back humming the same tune, but the fact is those Generals herd you around like sheep. And if you were the only ones to suffer, that would be your lookout. But innocent people get it in the neck too: I should have my baby by my side, but I had to give him up to the orphanage. If I'm leading this life it's all down to this copping war that you people don't know how to end. [...] He left me when I was five months

pregnant. After a while I couldn't disguise it, and when my father realised, he threw me out. So the war's fingered my life too.

(pp. 36–7; 38–9)

But this story of the illicit love of a motherless middle-class girl for a soldier, her subsequent pregnancy and disgrace, and her abandonment in the face of war, is also a stock of the romantic tradition. Even in the 1890s Leopoldo Alas was parodying just such a story line in his *Doña Berta*. The literary frame of the play, therefore, as well as its historical one, is defined by the sentimental commonplace. And perhaps the Daifa/ Courtesan herself is adept at manipulating these sentimental codes: certainly the other prostitutes regard her letter as a 'textbook' example of a letter from a fallen woman to her father, and perhaps this is indeed the way we are meant to read it, as a disingenuous and fabricated pretence at sorrow and regret. Some of her own statements – 'This letter would make a rock weep' – support this idea. But as the Daifa/Courtesan tears her hair out and sobs with grief on learning of her father's death (a grief unmitigated by the promise of an inheritance), on what basis do we dismiss her reaction as hysterical and insincere? Visually, the situation is ridiculous, as in her frenzy her hair flies loose and her skirt rides up to reveal her suspenders. But the fact that she is grief-stricken, in spite of the fact that her father's death releases her from her present situation, reveals her actions and her words to have been a product of naivety and perhaps stupidity rather than conscious malice. Unlike Juanito/Johnny, the Daifa/Courtesan has remained wedded to myth and glory, impressed by the soldier's medals, hoping her fiancé died bravely, trusting in the benevolent forgiveness of her father. A father who, let's not forget, is surely the most esperpentic character of the play. Juanito's coldness in the face of her grief is perhaps the reaction of a man inoculated by the bombastic rhetoric of war against contrived expressions of emotion, making him an amoral cynic (Cardona and Zahareas 1970, 216). This cynicism, so often assumed to be in the eye of the dramatist who renders her grief visually ludicrous, is powerfully offset against the emotional intensity beneath it. The final scene therefore brings together highly disparate and contrasting elements: it is deeply emotional but it gives the audience none of the satisfaction of complacent mawkishness or easy moralising, for these are sentimental reactions that also rely on cliché and bluster.

Las galas/Finery, then, is a play about the assumption of cultural values which are shown to be impoverished and self-interested. The emphasis on cliché is a significant manifestation of this theme, but the central visual motif is of course the symbolic suit of clothes. As John Lyon notes, 'Valle-Inclán was not much given to the use of dramatic symbolism, in the sense of events which have both structural importance for the action and metaphorical importance for the wider meaning of the play. *Las galas del difunto* is unusual in that it is constructed around such a symbolic event: the changing of the clothes' (1983, 138–39). It is this changing of the clothes that points to the importance of assumed roles and identities within the play, and to the superficiality of both the characters and their social environment. Clothes are twice evoked in the context of commercial transactions: Johnny Bluster pretends that he is a 'doing a deal' with the dead man when he exchanges his soldier's uniform for the chemist's suit, an exchange that also somehow furnishes him with the dead man's wallet; whilst the prostitute, dressed only in a blue robe and scarlet ribbon, has deposited her clothes with the brothel's madam as a surety against a loan. Valle-Inclán was contemptuous of the commercial ethos at the heart of modern bourgeois society, and the association of trade with thievery and prostitution is everywhere to be found in his work. The status associated with the suit is not only reflected in Juanito's desire for it, but in the Chemist's own implied pride in his ironed shirt, the top-quality fabric of his suit, and the new boots that chirrup like two crickets. Johnny wants the suit because of what it represents in social and economic terms; the Courtesan's clothes are both evidence of a former life (as the respectable daughter of a chemist) and her opportunity to forge a new life (because once she has recovered them she can move on). Like Juanito/Johnny, she is also a down-and-out figure in search of an assumed identity. In both cases it is stated or implied that the characters seek respectability, though in fact neither of them has any intention of living anywhere but among thieves and prostitutes – the implication being that this is all society has to offer. The assumption of a certain code of dress allows the characters to become mimics, just as the brothel mimics the convent by imitating its structures while lacking its moral core. But in all this mimicry the original model is either itself deformed or is nowhere to be found.

Johnny is 'transfigured by the dead man's clothes','but the transfiguration is decidedly sinister: 'His head is bare; the moonlight gives him a greenish halo' (p. 65). He becomes at once more markedly theatrical, greeting the other soldiers with a flourish and bursting in on Doña Terita with a 'stagey and outrageous bow' (p. 79). This staginess is reflected in frequent references to bullfighting, a recurrent source of images in Valle-Inclán's work, as Francisco Ynduráin has observed:

> The bullfight, in all its Spanishness, furnished [Valle-Inclán] with a great variety of images: he used these to capture the gestures and expressions, the bragging nerve bordering on bravado, and the vulgar, posturing theatricality associated with the event and all that comes with it. He created, in other words, a distorted caricature.
>
> (1969, 36)

This bullfighting motif, also heavily present in *Capitán/Captain*, is enhanced in *Las galas/Finery* by numerous references to dancing: not least among these is the kitsch and mannered angel gracing a basin of holy water in Doña Terita's bedroom, with 'its pink calves […] crossed as if it were dancing the bolero' (p. 79). Juanito himself 'struts and swaggers like a cockerel around the Chemist's Wife, pretending to dance and play the castanets' (p. 83), which provokes her into crying that 'Satan is among us! He is dancing around me beating his black wings!' (p. 85) There is considerable bathos in this comically sinister image of Satan dancing and whirling around the Chemist's Wife; in a similarly comical vein, the Cross-Eyed Aragonese mockingly responds to Galician Pedro's superstitious fear of death by asking whether 'this world and the next dance cheek to cheek' (p. 65). Bullfighting and dancing are relentlessly associated, in other words, with vulgar populism or conventional tweeness. Religious images – the halo, the angel, Satan and the spirit world, not to mention the graveyard and the 'necromancer's eye' of the chemist's window – are more superstitious or magical than they are moral or theological, and they are woven into a play that emphasizes performance, with all the macabre results that we might expect of such a combination. It also brings us back to the Don Juan legend, which consistently emphasizes Don Juan's posturing in the face of death.

Dru Dougherty asserts that Juanito/Johnny is 'a diminished figure, a Don Juan whose indomitable spirit is cheapened before our eyes by his comical gesticulations' (1980, 53). But Juanito/Johnny is not *just* a Don Juan figure; he is also a wan repatriated soldier abandoned to his fate by a corrupt institution. There are therefore very specific social and historical reasons for his metamorphosis from the latter into the former. Furthermore, though Juanito/Johnny blusters and postures he does not just gesticulate: he also acts; that is, he takes action. In the end Don Juan's 'indomitable spirit' is not cheapened by this version of the legend any more or less than by any other. The 'ventolera' or 'bluster' of his name evokes both shallowness and violence, a shallowness symbolised by the assumed suit of clothes, and a violence sanctioned in war but hypocritically punishable in peace:

PEDRO MASIDE	Yo, por mi parte, no. Para pelear con hombres, cuenta conmigo, pero no para despojar muertos.
JUANITO VENTOLERA	¿Pues qué otra cosa se hacía en campaña?
PEDRO MASIDE	No es lo mismo.
FRANCO RICOTE	Claramente que no. En un camposanto la sepultura es tierra sagrada.
JUANITO VENTOLERA	¡No se me había ocurrido este escrúpulo!
GALICIAN PEDRO	You can count me out. I'll fight the living, but you won't catch me robbing the dead.
JOHNNY BLUSTER	What was it we were doing in Cuba then?
GALICIAN PEDRO	That was different.
FRANCO THE SOUTHERNER	Of course it was. In a graveyard tombs are sacred.
JOHNNY BLUSTER	What fine scruples! I hadn't thought of that.

(pp. 60–1)

Don Juan's role has always been to challenge the hypocrisy of society; though this Don Juan is never allowed to be more than the society he challenges, he is not less than it either. By allowing Juanito/Johnny a measure of humanity, and by testing our emotional responses to the story of the Daifa/Courtesan, Valle-Inclán brings into sharper relief the social, historical and cultural context that determines their actions.

La hija del capitán/The Captain's Daughter

The last of the *esperpentos* to be written for the theatre, *La hija del capitán/The Captain's Daughter* is the most historically and politically oriented of Valle-Inclán's dramatic works. Published first in Buenos Aires in 1927 and in a slightly revised version a few months later in Madrid, Valle-Inclán set the action in the fictional land of Tartarinesia, removing all local references in an attempt to avoid the Spanish censor. In spite of his efforts, the play was withdrawn from circulation in Spain almost immediately, on the grounds that it offended morality and 'las buenas costumbres' [common decency] (Cardona and Zahareas 1970, 198).

It was no wonder the authorities withdrew the play, though they disingenuously claimed it was for moral rather than political reasons: *La hija del capitán/The Captain's Daughter* is an overt satire of the rise to power of General Primo de Rivera in 1923. To emphasise the corruption of the military and enhance the grotesque quality of events, Valle-Inclán draws on an earlier, unconnected incident that had become known in the newspapers as 'el crimen del capitán Sánchez' [the crime of Captain Sánchez]. This news story, which broke in 1913, told of the murder by a Spanish army captain and his daughter of a man who had last been seen gambling at the Círculo de Bellas Artes, a cultural institution and members' club housed in a fine Art Deco building on the corner of Madrid's Calle Alcalá and new Gran Vía (a club which, incidentally, became notorious for its raucous carnival festivities in the run-up to the Martes de carnaval or Mardi Gras). The story became ever more sensational as it was claimed that the captain and his daughter were having incestuous relations; that the murder was committed out of jealousy; and that the body had been dismembered and served up at the soldiers' mess. The army was accused of covering up the story to protect its own reputation. Although this story had no connection to Primo de Rivera, it served to establish a fictional chain of events that emphasised both the army's corruption and the hollowness of its claims to honour and patriotism.

Cliché and bluster are no less significant to *Capitán/Captain* than they were to *Las galas/Finery,* as we are exposed directly to the empty military bombast represented visually by Juanito's medals. Valle chooses not to make the Captain responsible for the murder that takes place in the play, however, attributing it instead to the daughter's jealous former lover, establishing in this way the arbitrary nature of the subsequent chain of events. The gruesome murder that has earned the Captain the nickname 'Chuletas de Sargento' (Captain Cutlets the Butcher) has taken place before the action of the play begins. We are told in scene one that the Captain's daughter, Sinibalda, has been prostituted to the General to get him off the hook; Sini has agreed to this because the General is rich and can keep her in the lap of luxury. In a fit of jealousy Sini's former lover, a lowly organ grinder, decides to kill the General but accidentally stabs one of his cronies, the Pollo de Cartagena/Spring Chicken, instead. Sini robs the dead man of his wallet, which happens to contain compromising documents belonging to the General. In an attempt to save his own reputation, the General silences the ensuing newspaper campaign against him by staging a military coup, amid protestations of military honour. Within the large cast of characters are representatives of the worlds of politics, journalism, the military, and the criminal underworld, but this last ultimately defines the other three. With a use of language perhaps more colourfully vulgar than in any other play, the characters' names and modes of expression underscore their basic dishonesty. There are no redeemable characters in this story: from the lowliest to the highest members of society, society operates on greed and self-interest. As John Lyon succinctly puts it, 'the implication is that the nation gets the government it deserves' (1983, 145).

If *Las galas/Finery* makes us view a potentially moving story through the distancing lens of the *esperpento*, the story of *Capitán/Captain* is already a tragic farce. Unusually, Valle dispenses with the literary context and relies instead on journalistic sources and Primo de Rivera's written declarations for both information and parody. As Cardona and Zahareas tell us, some of the most preposterous and rhetorical statements in the play are in fact direct quotes from Primo himself, who was known for his rather overblown communiqués (1970, 209). There are also a number of allusions to real events that a contemporary audience would doubtless have understood, though they don't always make sense in the context of the play's action: for example, the closure of Parliament is alluded to twice before the General has actually staged his coup; the General addresses his statement of patriotic duty to an invisible 'señora' (perhaps the Queen consort, Victoria of Battenberg, who was critical of Primo's suspension of parliamentary democracy (Cardona and Zahareas 1970, 209)); and he alludes to the words of an 'August Personage' who is, presumably, Primo himself. The play, in its final version, is also filled with references to geographical and cultural landmarks of the capital city, including the Gran Peña building, the Círculo de Bellas Artes, the Teatro Apolo, the Calle de la Montera, the area of Madrid briefly known as Madrid Moderno, and so on. The play was evidently written with a contemporary audience in mind, though its critique of the powerbrokers in society transcends its immediate context.

The play's emphasis on the present moment does not prevent Valle-Inclán from saturating it with references to the past. Many of these are implicit in the landscape of Madrid, not least the frequent allusions to Madrid Moderno. Though at first it might seem to refer to the 19th century expansion of the city, including the creation of its principal commercial and financial districts and new residential neighbourhoods, in fact it refers more specifically to a particular residential area within this *ensanche* or expansion. Constructed in the late 19th century on the site of one of Madrid's ancient barrios, Madrid Moderno (now on the edge of the Barrio de Salamanca) was characterized by small private residences (*hoteles*) built in *neo-mudéjar* style with large overhanging balconies or bay windows. The project was a political one inasmuch as it was intended, with its emphasis on the private individual, to be both the urban realization of Liberal values and the most 'European' of all Madrid's neighbourhoods. Indeed, the streets of the new area were dubbed with the names of such eminent 19th century Liberal politicians as Emilio Castelar, Roberto Aguilera (now the Calle Londres), and Segismundo Moret (now the Calle de Roma). It is perhaps the deliberate conflation of liberal and bourgeois values in this area of Madrid that allowed Valle-Inclán to inextricably associate the ideology of one with the culture of the other throughout his career. He was not the only one to be disheartened by the suburban architecture of Madrid Moderno: in his novel *La voluntad* (1902), the writer José Martínez Ruiz ("Azorín") scathingly described the 'diminutos hoteles' [diminutive private residences] he saw amassed near to the city's Ventas bullring,

> [...] en pintarrajeado conjunto de muros chafarrinados en viras rojas y amarillentas, balaustradas con jarrones, cristales azules y verdes, cupulillas, sórdidas ventanas, techumbres encarnadas y negras... todo chillón, pequeño, presuntuoso, procaz, frágil, de un mal gusto agresivo, de una vanidad cacareante, propia de un pueblo de tenderos y burócratas.

> [...] in a daubed assortment of walls blotted with red and streaked with yellow, balustrades with Grecian urns, blue and green stained glass, little domes and squalid windows, obscene rooves in red and black... everything is gaudy, petty, presumptuous, insolent, insubstantial, in aggressively bad taste, braggingly self-important, fit for a community of shopkeepers and bureaucrats.

(1902, 255)

Valle-Inclán's description of a 'calle jaulera de minúsculos hoteles' [cagey street of dolls' houses] (p. 103) expresses the same contempt for these private bourgeois residences. Madrid Moderno therefore becomes something of a metonym for Liberal ideology within the play, as the playwright makes ironic reference to the bourgeois ethos encapsulated in its architecture.

Though the play is a satire of Primo de Rivera and the military culture he represents, it is therefore in no way a defence of the parliamentary democracy or reigning liberal ideology that he did away with. Valle-Inclán's political changes of heart are notorious, but one ideology he was never tempted by was the liberal. In the early part of his career he identified with the ultra-conservative Carlists, an identification that Francisco Umbral dismisses as mere 'antimadrileñismo' [hostility towards Madrid] (58). Later in life he became a Socialist and Republican, but even in the midst of the Second Republic he expressed admiration for the grand historical vision of Mussolini's Fascism (Santos Zas 2010, 248). He was able to admire such a diverse range of political ideologies because they each in their own way aspired to something more or something other than the commercial ethos and bourgeois individualism that characterised Liberalism, particularly in the electorally corrupt and hypocritical form it had taken in Spain since the Restoration in 1875. Though the references to it are more implicit, *Capitán/Captain* is in many ways as much a critique of the power base that Primo swept aside as it is of Primo himself. This critique emerges not only in the repeated references to Madrid Moderno, but also in the allusions to Spain's corrupt institutions, to the 'gran liberal' the Conde de Romanones (Umbral 1998, 69), and in the atmosphere of political inactivity and cultural inanity that precedes the General's coup. The notes to the play give further information on each of these references to the state of affairs on the eve of the General's coup, but suffice it to say that Valle's political satire extended further than the military regime.

The play's preoccupation with history is further evident in the evocation of Spain's colonial past. It is significant in this context that both the General and the Captain should have spent time serving in Cuba. The *loro ultramarino* [imported parrot] and the *mucama mandinga* [mandinka maid] both testify to this, as do the colonial souvenirs that adorn the Captain's house:

Lacas chinescas y caracoles marinos, conchas perleras, coquitos labrados, ramas de madrépora y coral, difunden en la sala nostalgias coloniales de islas opulentas: Sobre la consola y por las rinconeras vestidas con tapetillos de primor casero, eran faustos y fábulas del trópico.

A room filled with burnished oriental figurines, sea conches, pearlescent shells, carved coconuts, branches of coral and madrepore. It has the nostalgically colonial air of an opulent isle. Set against the prim domestic cloths of the console and corner tables, the trinkets are exotically and ostentatiously tropical.

(pp. 112–3)

Perhaps not surprisingly, the wars that ended Spain's colonial occupation of Cuba and which formed the backdrop to *Las galas/Finery* are also an important historical reference point in the play. The General is described with great sarcasm as 'an illustrious veteran, supremo of the minor skirmish and suppressor of the folk hero' (p. 113; the folk hero in question is the Cuban patriot, Periquito Pérez). It is not only military figures that are evoked sarcastically in this context, however: the owner of the fictional newspaper of *El Constitucional*, Don Alfredo Toledano, he is said to have raised funds for soldiers returning from the war by setting up a charity 'devoted entirely to the needs of high-ranking officers' (p. 145). The first accounts of the terrible physical state in which returning soldiers found themselves provoked a series of charitable campaigns in the press to raise funds on their behalf (Núñez 1999, 35), but Valle-Inclán seems to be taking an ironic view of these campaigns, suggesting that they were fraudulent and exploitative. Don Alfredo's charitable enterprise, which only 'aids' those of high rank, is presumably of the same order. Whilst the loss of the colonies in 1898 is not the historical frame within which the play's action occurs, Valle-Inclán contextualises the contemporary events that are the target of his satire through a network of allusions, ideological and historical, to the past. The army's conduct in the present is linked to the events of the past, allowing each to throw light on the other and establishing a causal chain between then and now.

As John Lyon observes, in spite of its title the play's emphasis is more collective than individual, depicting bodies and institutions that operate unscrupulously and in their own interest, and dispensing with the figure of the tarnished hero. The Captain's daughter is perhaps singled out in the title because she is implicated in all stages of the action, from the original crime that earned her father the nickname 'Captain Cutlets' and which led to her *concubinage*, to the final scene where she comments wryly:

> ¡Carajeta, si [el Pollo] no la diña, la hubiera diñado la Madre Patria! De risa me escacho!

> Christ, if [the Spring Chicken] hadn't carked it the Motherland would have! It's so funny I could wet myself!

> (p. 173)

This idea that if he hadn't 'carked it the Motherland would have' encapsulates very succinctly the play's emphasis on the arbitrary nature of events on the one hand, and their manipulation on the other. The Spring Chicken is killed not only accidentally but absurdly by the organ grinder, whose actions couldn't have been justified even if he'd got the right victim; but this accident presents Sini with an opportunity which is in turn exploited by others in a position to benefit from the General's disgrace. The General is equally opportunistic in turn, mounting his bid for power (in the name of the 'Motherland') on the back of this unsavoury turn of events. The fact that neither the Captain nor the General is actually responsible for the Spring Chicken's death only highlights the extent to which the various players – to echo the play's gambling motif – take advantage of the hand they are played by circumstance. The emphasis then is on a network of characters rather than on individuals, but within this network Sini functions as a central figure around whom the action coalesces, though she is not endowed with any of the normal distinguishing properties of a heroine or even a protagonist. She has the same assertiveness as Juanito Ventolera/Johnny Bluster but in her case it is less convincing or justifiable, as she consistently overeggs her claim to be a victim. This victim mentality is a rare psychological trait in one of Valle-Inclán's esperpentic characters, and it serves not to rouse our sympathy but to do the opposite. Her accusations of ill treatment by her father, though not untruthful, come too soon after a dialogue which reveals her as an unscrupulous gold digger to be very compelling. In short, if Juanito/Johnny was no better and no worse than the society around him, this is perhaps even truer of La Sini, who never carried any mythical baggage in the first place.

If a tarnished hero does remain in the play it is of course in the figure of the General: like Juanito/Johnny or Friolera, he forms the centrepoint for the *esperpento*'s classic oppositional dynamic between myth and reality. The *esperpento* brings a distorted reality to myths of grandeur – tragic, heroic, archetypal – and reveals either the inadequacy of the myth or the inadequacy of the times, people or institutions to receive the myth. But in this case, interestingly, the myth is travelling in the opposite direction: rather than encapsulate an archetype of a former age, the General is instead a myth in the making: 'Un Príncipe de la Milicia levanta su espada victoriosa y sus luces inundan los corazones de las madres españolas!' [A Prince of the Celestial Army brandishes his sword of victory and it casts a penetrating light into the hearts of Spanish mothers!] (p. 168). There is also an element of this in *Don Friolera/ Mr Punch*, in which an epilogue to the play imagines a popular ballad exalting the wife-murdering lieutenant and sensationalising his exploits. In each case Valle-Inclán is concerned with exposing the empty bombast and dangerously self-aggrandising rhetoric that allows for the creation or continuity of degraded myths.

Like *Las galas/Finery, Capitán/Captain* makes use of a number of motifs that enhance its thematic concerns. Bullfighting and gambling provide numerous images and turns of phrase within the play, not only evoking a masculine world of *juerga* [benders], but also lending the action a sense of both ritual and chance. The language of the play is almost ecstatically varied in register and takes particular delight in highlighting incongruities (this is also evident in the names of many of the characters, whose apparent respectability is undermined by names that imply the opposite). The characters' speech weaves together unusual, often obscure vocabulary, literary allusions and complex images with crude and colloquial language which is nevertheless always more eccentric than obscene. The overall effect is expressionistic, in the sense that it relies on forceful contrast, but also impressionistic, in the sense that meaning plays second fiddle to effect. It is less about defining concrete meanings or recreating accurate modes of speech than it is about creating a mode of expression that highlights the pettiness, vulgarity, self-importance, greed, irresponsibility, insincerity and ambition of all the play's characters, regardless of their status or place in society. The emphasis on incongruity and contrast in the use of register creates a peculiarly sarcastic tone that permeates the dialogue.

The translation of these two plays into English and their publication in a bilingual edition will, I hope, allow readers with a variety of academic interests to appreciate the immense literary and dramatic value of these *esperpentos*, as well as the challenges faced by the translator (see the Translator's Note). Both plays extend the theoretical definition of the *esperpento* as Valle-Inclán outlined it in *Luces/Lights* and *Friolera/ Mr Punch*: in the case of *Las galas/Finery*, by bringing emotion and sentimentality into particularly forceful contrast; and in the case of *Capitán/Captain*, by dispensing with the literary frame of reference and the fallen mythical hero in favour of a collective protagonist in a roaring political satire.

BIBLIOGRAPHY

Avalle-Arce, J. B. 1959. La esperpentización de *Don Juan Tenorio*, *Hispanófila*, 7, 29–39.

Aznar Soler, M. 1992a. *Valle-Inclán, Rivas Cherif y la renovación teatral española (1907–1936)*. Sant Cugat del Vallès, Barcelona: Cop d'Idees: Taller d'Investigacions Valleinclanianes.

Aznar Soler, M. 1992b. *Guía de lectura de Martes de Carnaval*. Barcelona: Anthropos.

Cardona, R. and Zahareas, A. 1970. *Visión del Esperpento: Teoría y práctica en los esperpentos de Valle-Inclán*. Madrid: Castalia.

Cowans, J. (ed.). 2003. *Modern Spain: A Documentary History*. 'The Barcelona Manifesto', transl. D. F. Ratcliff. Philadelphia: University of Pennsylvania Press.

Dougherty, D. 1980. The Tragicomic Don Juan: Valle-Inclán's *Esperpento de las galas del difunto (The Dead Man's Duds)*, *Modern Drama* XXIII: 1 (March), 44–57.

Fox, D. 1986. *Kings in Calderón: A Study in Characterization and Political Theory*. London: Tamesis.

Gay, J. 1728. *The Beggar's Opera*, ed. by Bryan Loughrey and T. O. Treadwell. London: Penguin, 1986.

Levy, A. 2004. *Small Island*. London: Review.

Lima, R. 2003. *The Dramatic World of Valle-Inclán*. Woodbridge: Tamesis.

Lyon, J. 1983. *The Theatre of Valle-Inclán*. Cambridge: Cambridge University Press.

Mandel, O. (ed.). 1963. *The Theatre of Don Juan: A Collection of Plays and Views 1630–1963*. Nebraska: University of Nebraska Press.

Martínez Ruiz, J. ("Azorín"). 1902. *La voluntad*, ed. by María Martínez del Portal. Madrid: Cátedra, 1997.

Nuñez Florencio, R. 1999. El drama de la repatriación, *Militaria, Revista de cultura militar* 13, 33–45.

Rubio Jiménez, J. (ed.). 2008. *Martes de carnaval*. Madrid: Espasa Calpe.

Santos Zas, M. and the Grupo de Investigación Valle-Inclán de la Universidade de Santiago de Compostela. 2010. *Todo Valle-Inclán en Roma (1933–1936). Edición, anotación, índices y facsímiles*. Santiago de Compostela: USC/ Deputación de Pontevedra.

Senabre, R. (ed.). 1990. *Martes de carnaval*. Madrid: Espasa Calpe.

Thomas, H. 2001. *The Spanish Civil War* (revised edition). New York: Modern Library.

Umbral, F. 1998. *Valle-Inclán. Los botines blancos de piqué.* Barcelona: Planeta.

Valle-Inclán, J. del. 2007. 'Guía de lectura' to *Luces de Bohemia*, ed. by A. Zamora Vicente. Madrid: Espasa Calpe.

Valle-Inclán, R. del. *Luces de Bohemia.* 1924. ed. A. Zamora Vicente, 'Guía de lectura' and Glossary Joaquín del Valle-Inclán. Madrid: Espasa Calpe, 2007.

Valle-Inclán, R. del. *Martes de Carnaval. Esperpentos.* 1930. ed. and intro. R. Senabre. Madrid: Espasa Calpe, 1990.

Valle-Inclán, R. del. *Esperpento de los cuernos de Don Friolera/ The Grotesque Farce of Mr Punch the Cuckold.* 1921. trans. D. Keown and R. Warner. Warminster: Aris & Phillips, 1991.

Varela Ortega, J. *et al.* 2001. *El poder de la influencia: geografía del caciquismo en España 1875–1923.* Madrid: Marcial Pons.

Walters, D. G. 2002. *The Cambridge Introduction to Spanish Poetry: Spain and Spanish America.* Cambridge: Cambridge University Press.

Wodehouse, P. G. 1954. *Jeeves and the Feudal Spirit.* London: Arrow Books, 2008.

Ynduráin, F. 1969. *Valle-Inclán. Tres estudios.* Santander: La Isla de los Ratones.

Zorrilla, J. 1844. *Don Juan Tenorio*, ed. by Aniano Peña. Madrid: Cátedra, 2012.

Websites consulted

Twists, Slug and Roscoes: A Glossary of Hardboiled Slang
http://www.miskatonic.org/slang.html

Jumieka Langwij
http://www.jumieka.com/

The Urban Dictionary
www.urbandictionary.com

En la prensa de aquel día: El blog de la prensa antigua
http://periodicosregalo.blogspot.com/2011/11/revista-blanco-y-negro-desde-1891.html

Wikipedia, 'Digger slang'
www.wikipedia.com

LAS GALAS DEL DIFUNTO

THE DEAD MAN'S FINERY

Dramatis Personae

La BRUJA de los mandados en la casa llana
Una DAIFA y JUANITO VENTOLERA, pistolo repatriado
Un GALOPÍN, mancebo de botica
El BOTICARIO Don Sócrates Galindo y Doña Terita la BOTICARIA
Tres soldados de rayadillo: PEDRO MASIDE, FRANCO RICOTE y EL BIZCO
MALUENDA
Un SACRISTÁN y un RAPISTA
La MADRE Celestina y las niñas del pecado

ESCENA PRIMERA

La casa del pecado, en un enredo de callejones, cerca del muelle viejo. Prima noche. Luces de la marina. Cantos remotos en un cafetín. Guiños de las estrellas. Pisadas de zuecos. Brilla la luna en las losas mojadas de la acera: Tapadillo de la Carmelitana: Sala baja con papel floreado: Dos puertas azules, entornadas sobre dos alcobas: En el fondo, las camas tendidas con majas colchas portuguesas: En el reflejo del quinqué, LA DAIFA pelinegra, con un lazo detonante en el moño, cierra el sobre de una carta: Luce en la mejilla el rizo de un lunar. A LA BRUJA que se recose el zancajo en el fondo mal alumbrado de una escalerilla, hizo seña mostrando la carta. La coima muerde la hebra, y se prende la aguja en el pecho.

LA BRUJA	¡Vamos a ese fin del mundo! ¡Si siquiera de tantas idas se sacase algún provecho!...
LA DAIFA	La carta va puesta como para conmover una peña.
LA BRUJA	¡Ay, qué viejo renegado! ¡Cuándo se lo llevará Satanás!...
LA DAIFA	Es muy contraria mi suerte.
LA BRUJA	¡Sí que lo es! ¡El padre acaudalado y la hija arrastrada!
LA DAIFA	¡Y tener que desearle la muerte para mejorar de conducta!

Dramatis Personae

A whorehouse WITCH, bawd and messenger
A COURTESAN[1] and JOHNNY BLUSTER, a veteran squaddie[2]
A CALLOW YOUTH, the CHEMIST's assistant
The CHEMIST Don Socrates and Doña Terita, the CHEMIST's wife
Three soldiers in striped uniforms: GALICIAN PEDRO, FRANCO THE SOUTHERNER, and the CROSS-EYED ARAGONESE[3]
A SEXTON and a BARBER
Celestina, the brothel's MADAM (known as the Mother Superior), and the daughters of sin

SCENE ONE

A brothel in a tangle of alleyways near the old harbour. Night has just fallen. Lights glisten from the marina. Distant sounds of singing from a tavern. Stars glitter up above. Clogs slap on the wet pavement, shimmering in the moonlight. A Carmelite brothel; a low-ceilinged room with flowered wallpaper; two blue doors, which open onto two bedrooms; in the background, beds with pretty Portuguese bedspreads. In the glow of the oil lamp the black-haired COURTESAN, with a dazzling ribbon in her hair, seals an envelope containing a letter; on her cheek is the round curl of a beauty spot. She waves the letter at the WITCH, who is darning her stockings in the dim stairway. The bawd[4] snaps the thread with her teeth, and slips the needle into her bodice.

WITCH	Back to that hellhole! Fat lot of good it'll do us.
COURTESAN	This letter would make a rock weep.
WITCH	Vile, disloyal old man! May he rot long and hard in hell!
COURTESAN	This might just save my skin. I've been so unfortunate![5]
WITCH	Unfortunate, yes! The father flush and the daughter in the gutter…!
COURTESAN	… Forced to wish him dead to improve her lot!

LA BRUJA	¡Si te vieras con capitales, era el ponerte de ama y dorarte de monedas, que el negocio lo puede! ¡Y no ser ingrata con una vida que te dio refugio en tu desgracia!
LA DAIFA	¡No habrá una peste negra que se lo lleve!
LA BRUJA	Tú llámale por la muerte, que mucho puede el deseo, y más si lo acompañas encendiéndole una vela a Patillas.
LA DAIFA	¡Renegado pensamiento! ¡Dejémosle vivir, que al fin es mi padre!
LA BRUJA	Para ti ha sido un verdugo.
LA DAIFA	¡Se le puso una venda de sangre considerando la deshonra de sus canas!
LA BRUJA	Pudo cubrirla, si tanto no le representase aflojar la mosca, pero la avaricia se lo come. ¿Espero respuesta de la carta?
LA DAIFA	Si te la da la tomas. Tienes que correr para no hallar la puerta cerrada.
LA BRUJA	Volaré.

La bruja encaperuzó el manto sobre las sienes y voló convertida en corneja. La daifa de la bata celeste y el lazo escarlata sale a la puerta haciendo la jarra, y permanece en el umbral mirando a la calle. Por la otra acera, un sorche repatriado, al que dicen JUANITO VENTOLERA.

LA DAIFA	¡Chis!... ¡Chis!...
JUANITO VENTOLERA	¿Es para mí ese reclamo, paloma?
LA DAIFA	¿No te gusto?
JUANITO VENTOLERA	¡Un pasmo! ¿No me ve usted, niña, con las patas colgando?
LA DAIFA	Pues atorníllate, pelmazo.
JUANITO VENTOLERA	¿Quiere usted fuera la llave de tuercas?
LA DAIFA	Ese timo es habanero.
JUANITO VENTOLERA	¿Conoce usted aquel país?
LA DAIFA	No lo conozco, pero tiene usted todo el hablar de los repatriados. ¡La propia pinta! ¿No lo es usted?

WITCH	If you had money, you could be mistress of this house and cover yourself in gold, because business is good! And don't you be ungrateful, because we took you in when you had nothing!
COURTESAN	I hope he dies of some seething canker!
WITCH	That's right, you call on death to take him. Wishes can be very powerful, especially if you light a candle to Old Nick.
COURTESAN	Such disloyalty! Let him live; he is my father, after all.
WITCH	Your executioner!
COURTESAN	The blood runs hot in his veins! The shame was too much for his venerable temples.
WITCH	He could have hushed it up, if greed hadn't devoured his miserly heart. Shall I wait for a reply?
COURTESAN	Yes, and if there is one take it. Run or he'll have locked the door.
WITCH	I'll fly.

The WITCH pulls the cloak up around her temples and, turning into a raven, flies away. The COURTESAN, in her sky-blue robe and scarlet ribbon, goes to the door and places her hand on her hip. She stands on the threshold looking out at the street. On the pavement opposite stands a veteran squaddie known as JOHNNY BLUSTER.

COURTESAN:	Psst!.... Hey!...
JOHNNY BLUSTER	Are you cooing at me, pigeon?
COURTESAN	Don't you like me?
JOHNNY BLUSTER	Like you! Can't you see my tongue hanging out?
COURTESAN	Well come on then, screw up your courage.
JOHNNY BLUSTER	You after my screwdriver?
COURTESAN	That quip stinks of Havana.
JOHNNY BLUSTER	You been there?
COURTESAN	No, but you sound just like all the soldiers back from Cuba. You look like one too! Are you a soldier?

JUANITO VENTOLERA	No más hace que tres horas. A las seis tocamos puerto.
LA DAIFA	¿En qué Regimiento estaba usted?
JUANITO VENTOLERA	Segunda Compañía de Lucena.
LA DAIFA	¡Segunda de Lucena! ¿Y usted, por un casual, habrá conocido a un punto practicante que llamaban Aureliano Iglesias?
JUANITO VENTOLERA	Buen punto estaba ése.
LA DAIFA	¿Le ha conocido usted, por un acaso? ¿No es una trola? ¿Le ha conocido?
JUANITO VENTOLERA	Bastante. Simpatizamos.
LA DAIFA	Era mi novio. Estábamos para casar.
JUANITO VENTOLERA	Pues aquí tiene usted su consuelo.
LA DAIFA	¿De verdad has conocido tú a Aureliano Iglesias?
JUANITO VENTOLERA	Y tanta verdad.
LA DAIFA	¿Sabes cómo murió?
JUANITO VENTOLERA	Como un valiente.
LA DAIFA	¡A los redaños que tenía, algunos mambises habrá tumbado!
JUANITO VENTOLERA	Muchos no habrán sido... Siempre se tira de lejos.
LA DAIFA	Pero alguno doblaría.
JUANITO VENTOLERA	Pudiera...
LA DAIFA	¿Tú no crees?...
JUANITO VENTOLERA	Allí solamente se busca el gasto de municiones. Es una cochina vergüenza aquella guerra. El soldado, si supiese su obligación y no fuese un paria, debería tirar sobre sus jefes.
LA DAIFA	Todos volvéis con la misma polca, pero ello es que os llevan y os traen como a borregos. Y si fueseis solos a pasar las penalidades, os estaría muy bien puesto. Pero las consecuencias alcanzan a los más inocentes, y un hijo que hoy estaría criándose a mi lado, lo tengo en la Maternidad. Esta vida en que me ves, se la debo a esa maldita guerra que no sabéis acabar.

JOHNNY BLUSTER	I was until three hours ago. We docked at six.
COURTESAN	What regiment were you in?
JOHNNY BLUSTER	The Second Company of Lucena.
COURTESAN	The Lucena Seconds! You didn't happen to know an active serviceman, one Aureliano Iglesias…?
JOHNNY BLUSTER	That troublemaker!
COURTESAN	You knew him, really? You're not having me on? You really knew him?
JOHNNY BLUSTER	I did. We clicked.
COURTESAN	He was my fiancé. We were about to get married.
JOHNNY BLUSTER	Well, here's your consolation prize.
COURTESAN	You honestly knew Aureliano Iglesias?
JOHNNY BLUSTER	I honestly did.
COURTESAN	Do you know how he died?
JOHNNY BLUSTER	Like a hero.
COURTESAN	He had the heart of a lion… I bet he doubled a few of those rebel *mambis*![6]
JOHNNY BLUSTER	Maybe… I doubt it… we had to shoot at them from a distance.
COURTESAN	He must have bent up one or two.
JOHNNY BLUSTER	It's possible.
COURTESAN	But not likely?
JOHNNY BLUSTER	The war in Cuba is just a waste of ammunition. It's a filthy disgrace. If soldiers weren't such bludgers and knew where their real duty lay, they'd turn their guns on the shiny arses in charge.
COURTESAN	You all come back humming the same tune, but the fact is those Generals herd you around like sheep. And if you were the only ones to suffer, that would be your lookout. But innocent people get it in the neck too: I should have my baby by my side, but I had to give him up to the orphanage. If I'm leading this life it's all down to this copping war that you people don't know how to end.

JUANITO VENTOLERA	Porque no se quiere. La guerra es un negocio de los galones. El soldado sólo sabe morir.
LA DAIFA	¡Como el mío! ¿Oye, tú, le envolverían en la bandera?
JUANITO VENTOLERA	No era para tanto. ¡La bandera! Pues no dice nada la gachí. La bandera es la oreja. ¡Esos honores se quedan para los jefes!
LA DAIFA	¿Y por eso tenéis todos tan mala voluntad a los galones?
JUANITO VENTOLERA	De esas camamas, al soldado poco se le da. ¡No robaran ellos como roban en el rancho y en el haber!...
LA DAIFA	Pues a tumbar galones. Pero todos lo dicen y ninguno lo hace.
JUANITO VENTOLERA	Alguno hay que lo hizo.
LA DAIFA	¿Tú, por ventura?
JUANITO VENTOLERA	Otro de mi cara.
LA DAIFA	Mírame en este ojo. Tú te has aguantado las bofetadas igual que todos. ¿De verdad has conocido a Aureliano Iglesias?
JUANITO VENTOLERA	¡De verdad!
LA DAIFA	¿Y le has visto caer propiamente?
JUANITO VENTOLERA	Propiamente.
LA DAIFA	¿En el campo?
JUANITO VENTOLERA	A mi lado, en la misma trinchera.
LA DAIFA	¿Con redaños?
JUANITO VENTOLERA	Cuando no queda otro remedio, todo quisque saca los redaños.
LA DAIFA	Se fue dejándome embarazada de cinco meses. Pasado un poco tiempo no pude tenerlo oculto, y al descubrirse, mi padre me echó al camino. Por donde también a mí me alcanza la guerra. ¿Tú de qué parte del mundo eres?
JUANITO VENTOLERA	De esta tierra.
LA DAIFA	No lo pareces.
JUANITO VENTOLERA	¿Pues de dónde me das?

JOHNNY BLUSTER	Because nobody wants it to end. For the Generals, war is business. Soldiers only know how to die.
COURTESAN	Like my soldier! Hey, tell me, did they drape his coffin with the flag?
JOHNNY BLUSTER	The flag? Hark at you! Do nags get rosettes?[7] Hardly! Only top brass get honours like that!
COURTESAN	And that's why you all hate them so much?
JOHNNY BLUSTER	Niceties[8] like that aren't for the soldiers. They rob us of those like they rob us in the mess or rob us of our wages.
COURTESAN	Well down with the top brass. But everybody says it and nobody does anything about it.
JOHNNY BLUSTER	I know somebody that might have.
COURTESAN	Was it you, by any chance?
JOHNNY BLUSTER	Someone who looked like me.
COURTESAN	Look me in the eye. You've had it tough like everybody else. Did you really, truly know Aureliano Iglesias?
JOHNNY BLUSTER	Really, truly.
COURTESAN	And you saw him die as he should?
JOHNNY BLUSTER	As he should.
COURTESAN	On the battlefield?
JOHNNY BLUSTER	Right next to me, in the trench.
COURTESAN	And he had balls?
JOHNNY BLUSTER	When there's no other choice, everyone's got balls.
COURTESAN	He left me when I was five months pregnant. After a while I couldn't disguise it, and when my father realised, he threw me out. So the war's fingered my life too. Where are you from?
JOHNNY BLUSTER	From around here.
COURTESAN	I wouldn't have guessed.
JOHNNY BLUSTER	Where would you say I was from?

LA DAIFA	Cuatro leguas arriba de los Infiernos. O mucho me engaño, o tú eres otro Ravachol.
JUANITO VENTOLERA	¿Pues qué me ves?
LA DAIFA	La punta del rabo.
JUANITO VENTOLERA	Siento no agradarte, paloma. Lo siento de veras.
LA DAIFA	¿Quién te ha dicho que no me agradas? Tanto me agradas, y si quieres convidar, puedes hacerlo.
JUANITO VENTOLERA	Estoy sin plata.
LA DAIFA	Algo tendrás.
JUANITO VENTOLERA	El corazón para quererte, niña.
LA DAIFA	¿Ni siquiera tienes un duro romanonista?
JUANITO VENTOLERA	Ni eso.
LA DAIFA	¿Ni una beata para convidar?
JUANITO VENTOLERA	Pelado al cero, niña.
LA DAIFA	¡Más que pelado! ¡Calvorota!
JUANITO VENTOLERA	Es el premio que hallamos al final de la campaña. ¡Y aún nos piden ser héroes!
LA DAIFA	¡Cabritos sois!
JUANITO VENTOLERA	¡Y tan cabritos!

LA MADRE del prostíbulo aparece por la escalerilla, llenándola con el ruedo de sus faldas: Trae en la mano una palmatoria que le entrecruza la cara de reflejos. Detrás, en revuelo, bajan dos palomas. La dueña es obesa, grandota, con muchos peines y rizos: Un erisipel le repela las cejas.

LA MADRE	¿Vas a pasarte la noche con ese pelma? Métete dentro.
LA DAIFA	Ya has oído. ¡Que ahueques!
JUANITO VENTOLERA	¿Así me da usted boleta, morena? ¡Usted no quiere ver en mí al testamentario de Aureliano Iglesias!
LA DAIFA	¡Camelista! ¡Si al menos tuvieses para pagar la cama!

COURTESAN	Straight out of hell for all I know! You look just like that frenchie, the anarchist bandit, Ravachol.[9]
JOHNNY BLUSTER	So how do you like me?
COURTESAN	Like a dose of pox.
JOHNNY BLUSTER	I'm sorry you don't fancy me, pigeon. Really I am.
COURTESAN	Who says I don't? I do fancy you, and if you want to buy me a drink I won't say no.
JOHNNY BLUSTER	I'm broke.
COURTESAN	You must have some money tucked away.
JOHNNY BLUSTER	All I can give is my heart, precious.
COURTESAN	Not even a bit of loose change?[10]
JOHNNY BLUSTER	Not even that.
COURTESAN	Not even a *peseta* to buy me a drink?
JOHNNY BLUSTER	Nothing but the clothes on my back.
COURTESAN	You are on your uppers!
JOHNNY BLUSTER	It's the prize they give us at the end of the campaign. But they still expect us to behave like heroes!
COURTESAN	You're like lambs to the slaughter!
JOHNNY BLUSTER	Donkeys, more like.

The brothel's MADAM *appears in the stairway, filling it with the circumference of her skirts. She holds a candlestick in her hand: light and shadow play across her face. Behind her, a commotion of flapping wings as two doves fly down from the roof. The Mother Superior is large and very fat, her hair full of combs and curls. She has lost her eyebrows to a nasty infection of the skin.*

MADAM	Are you spending the night with this reprobate? Get inside.
COURTESAN	You heard what she said. Go on, clear off!
JOHNNY BLUSTER	So that's how we say goodnight now, is it? I suppose you don't want to know what Aureliano left you in his will!
COURTESAN	Grifter! If only you had enough to pay for tonight!

JUANITO VENTOLERA	Nada tengo.
LA DAIFA	Pues la cama es una beata. Dirás que no la tienes, con las cruces que llevas en el pecho. ¡Alguna será pensionada!
JUANITO VENTOLERA	Te hago donación de todo el tinglado.
LA DAIFA	Gracias.
JUANITO VENTOLERA	Son las que me cuelgan.
LA MADRE	Ernestina, basta de pelma.
LA DAIFA	Es un amigo de mi Aureliano.
JUANITO VENTOLERA	¿Hacemos changa, negra?
LA DAIFA	¿Y si te tomase la palabra?
JUANITO VENTOLERA	Por tomada. Me das la dormida y te cuelgas este calvario.
LA DAIFA	¡Pss!... No me convence.
JUANITO VENTOLERA	Te adornas la espetera.
LA DAIFA	¡Guasista!
JUANITO VENTOLERA	Salte un paso que te lo cuelgo.
LA DAIFA	El ama está alerta. ¿Qué medalla es ésta?
JUANITO VENTOLERA	Sufrimientos por la Patria.
LA DAIFA	¡Hay que ver!... ¿Y ésta?
JUANITO VENTOLERA	Del Mérito.
LA DAIFA	¡Has sido un héroe!
JUANITO VENTOLERA	¡Un cabrón!
LA DAIFA	¡Me estás cayendo la mar simpático! ¿Y esta cruz?
JUANITO VENTOLERA	De Doña Virtudes. El lilailo que te haga tilín, te lo cuelgas. Como si te apetece todo el tinglado. ¡Mi palabra es de Alfonso!
LA DAIFA	Espera que nos conozcamos más.
JUANITO VENTOLERA	¿Y cuándo va a ser ese conocimiento?
LA DAIFA	Pásate por aquí la tarde del lunes, que me toca libre. Antes no vengas. Y aún mejor apaño será que me dejes la tarde libre. Ven por la noche, sobre esta hora... Si acaso te acuerdas.

JOHNNY BLUSTER	I'm cleaned out.
COURTESAN	Well it's one *peseta*. Don't tell me you can't afford it, with all those crosses and medals you've got hanging off you! One of them must earn you a pension!
JOHNNY BLUSTER	You can have the whole copping lot.
COURTESAN	Thanks!
JOHNNY BLUSTER	As you can see, I'm well hung!
MADAM	Ernestina, that's enough chat.
COURTESAN	He knew my Aureliano.
JOHNNY BLUSTER	So have we got a deal or not?
COURTESAN	Will you give me your word?
JOHNNY BLUSTER	Why not? Spend the night with me and this calvary of crosses is all yours.
COURTESAN	Hmm!... I'm not sure.
JOHNNY BLUSTER	Wear them on your chest! Can't hurt a girl like you to be well endowed…!
COURTESAN	Very funny!
JOHNNY BLUSTER	Get yourself over here gorgeous, and I'll pin one on you.
COURTESAN	The Mother Superior's watching. What did you get this medal for?
JOHNNY BLUSTER	Services to the Nation.
COURTESAN	Really! And this one?
JOHNNY BLUSTER	Meritorious Conduct.
COURTESAN	You are a hero!
JOHNNY BLUSTER	An idiot!
COURTESAN	I think I'm falling for you! And this one? What's this cross for?
JOHNNY BLUSTER	For being so copping virtuous. Have whichever trinket takes your fancy. Take the lot for all I care. My word is as good as the King's![11]
COURTESAN	Wait, we should get to know each other first.
JOHNNY BLUSTER	Get to know each other… when?
COURTESAN	Come by on Monday afternoon; I'm free then. Don't come before. Better still, let me have the afternoon to myself and come in the evening, around this time… but I expect you'll forget.

JUANITO VENTOLERA	Me has puesto cadena.
LA MADRE	¡Ernestina!
LA DAIFA	El ama está echando café. Vete no más. Toma un recuerdo.

LA DAIFA se saca una horquilla del moño y se la ofrece con guiño chunguero. Éntrase, y desde el fondo de la sala se vuelve. El soldado todavía está en la acera. Alto, flaco, macilento, los ojos de fiebre, la manta terciada, el gorro en la oreja, la trasquila en la sien. El tinglado de cruces y medallas daba sus brillos buhoneros.

JOHNNY BLUSTER	I'll consider it my sacred duty to remember.
MADAM	Ernestina!
COURTESAN	She's about to blow; you'd better scarper. Here's something to remember me by.

The COURTESAN takes a hairpin out of her chignon and hands it to him with a mischievous wink. She goes inside, turning round when she reaches the far end of the room. The gunner is still standing on the pavement: tall, thin and wan, his eyes febrile, his cloak lopsided, his cap tilted to one side, his head shorn above the temples. The jumble of crosses and medals glitters on his uniform like a pedlar's wares.

ESCENA SEGUNDA

Farmacia del licenciado Sócrates Galindo. LA BRUJA del tapadillo, con la carta de LA DAIFA, posa el vuelo en el relumbre de la pupila mágica, que proyecta sobre la acera el ojo del BOTICARIO. Por una punta del rebozo, las uñas negras, los dedos rayados del iris, oprimen la carta de la manflota. La mandadera mete la cabeza curuja por el vano de la puerta, pegada a un canto. Maja en el mortero un virote de mandilón y alpargatas.

LA BRUJA	Traigo una carta de aquella afligida para el viejo. Llámale.
EL GALOPÍN	Ha salido.
LA BRUJA	¡Raro se me hace! De ser un aparente, mal harías negándomelo. Mira, hijo, para que te crea, en un santiamén dos onzas de cornezuelo.
EL GALOPÍN	El cornezuelo no se despacha sin receta.
LA BRUJA	¡Adonde vas tú con ese miramiento! ¡Que no despacharéis pocas drogas sin receta! Anda, negro, y te las perronas.
EL GALOPÍN	¡Y me busco un compromiso, si cuadra!
LA BRUJA	¿Tampoco tomarás a tu cargo entregarle la carta al viejo?
EL GALOPÍN	Tampoco.
LA BRUJA	¡Hijo, eres propiamente una ortiga! La ley de los pobres es ayudarse.
EL GALOPÍN	¿Quiere usted encargarse del almirez y majar un rato?
LA BRUJA	¡Cuernos!
EL GALOPÍN	¡Los suyos!
LA BRUJA	¡Malhablado! ¿Adonde salió el patrón?
EL GALOPÍN	A entrevistarse con el alcalde.
LA BRUJA	¿Anda en justicias?
EL GALOPÍN	Le han puesto una brasa en el traste.
LA BRUJA	Explica esa picardía.

SCENE TWO

A CHEMIST's belonging to the honourable Don Socrates. In the window, from a glass-fronted medicine cabinet, shines a painted eye.[12] *The whorehouse WITCH, carrying the COURTESAN's letter, alights in its magical glare. Her blackened nails creep around the hem of her shawl: her fingers, clutching the prostitute's letter, are streaked with coloured light. The messenger sticks her owl's head around the doorframe. A young dimwit wearing overalls and espadrilles is pounding something in a mortar.*

WITCH	I've got a letter from that poor girl for the old man. Where is he?
CALLOW YOUTH	He's gone out.
WITCH	Is that so? Your nose is growing; don't deny it. Listen, son, so I know I can trust you, weigh me a couple of ounces of that ergot. Quick sticks!
CALLOW YOUTH	You need a prescription for ergot.
WITCH	What do you care about that? Don't tell me it's the first time you've dispensed drugs without a prescription! Come on now, and you can keep the change.
CALLOW YOUTH	It's more than my job's worth!
WITCH	Can I at least commission you to give this letter to the old man?
CALLOW YOUTH	No.
WITCH	You're a real gem, you are! The poor have a duty to one another!
CALLOW YOUTH	How about taking over the mortar and pounding for a while?
WITCH	Get stuffed!
CALLOW YOUTH	You get stuffed!
WITCH	Watch your mouth! Where did the boss go?
CALLOW YOUTH	To talk to the mayor.
WITCH	About a lawsuit?
CALLOW YOUTH	He's just got his gander up.
WITCH	What do you mean?

EL GALOPÍN	Le echaron un alojado, y anda en los pasos para que le rediman la carga.
LA BRUJA	¡Tío cicatero! ¿A qué hora cerráis?
EL GALOPÍN	A las nueve.
LA BRUJA	¿Vendrá antes?
EL GALOPÍN	Pudiera ser.
LA BRUJA	¿Por qué no te encargas tú de darle la carta? Me alargo a otro mandado, y vuelvo por la respuesta. Así la tiene meditada.

La trotaconventos entra a dejar la carta sobre el mostrador, y escapa arrebujándose: En la puerta, con arrecido de BRUJA zorrera, cruza por delante del BOTICARIO, que se queda suspenso, enarbolado el bastón sobre la encorujada, sin llegar a bajarlo.

| EL BOTICARIO | ¡Recoge esa carta! ¡No quiero recibirla! ¡Me mancharía las manos! ¡A la relajada que aquí te encamina, dile, de una vez para siempre, que no logrará conmover mi corazón! ¡Llévate ese papel, y remonta el vuelo, si no quieres que te queme las pezuñas! ¡Llévate ese papel, y no aparezcas más! |
| LA BRUJA | ¡Esa carta suplica una respuesta! |

EL BOTICARIO recoge la carta, que con rara sugestión acusa su cuadrilátero encima del mostrador, y la tira al arroyo.

LA BRUJA	¡Iscariote!
EL BOTICARIO	¡Emplumada!
LA BRUJA	¡Perro avariento, es una hija necesitada la que te implora! ¡Tu hija! ¡Corazón perverso, no desoigas la voz de la sangre!
EL BOTICARIO	Vienes mal guiada, serpiente. ¿De qué hija me hablas? Una tuve y se ha muerto. Los muertos no escriben cartas. ¡Retira ese papel de la calle, vieja maldita!
LA BRUJA	¡Guau! ¡Guau! Ahí se queda para tu sonrojo. Que lo recoja y lo lea el primero que pase.

CALLOW YOUTH	They've made him take in a lodger, and he's doing everything he can to get rid of him.
WITCH	Cheapskate! What time do you close?
CALLOW YOUTH	At nine.
WITCH	Will he be back before then?
CALLOW YOUTH	Maybe.
WITCH	Why don't you take charge of the letter? I've got another errand to run, but I'll be back to pick up his reply. That'll give him time to consider.

The procuress goes in and leaves the letter on the counter, then wraps herself up in her cloak to leave. The CHEMIST appears in the doorway; the crafty WITCH flits in front of him and he stands stock still, threatening her with his raised walking stick, but unable to bring it down on her owl's head.

CHEMIST	Take back that letter! I don't want it! I won't dirty my hands! Once and for all, tell that slattern that my heart will not yield! Get out of my sight, and take that bit of paper with you, or I'll roast your hooves on the fire! Take it away, and don't come back!
WITCH	That letter demands an answer!

The CHEMIST picks up the letter, which lies with a strangely emotive stubborn squareness on the counter. He throws it in the gutter.

WITCH	Judas!
CHEMIST	Crone!
WITCH	You avaricious dog, your daughter is desperate and she is begging you for help! Your own daughter! Open your heart to your own flesh and blood!
CHEMIST	You don't know what you're talking about, you snake. I don't have a daughter. I had one but she died. Dead people don't write letters. Go and fetch it off the street you old bitch, and leave me alone!
WITCH	Woof! Woof! It can stay there for all I care. Some passer-by can pick it up and read it, then you'll know what real shame is.

Se alejaba la voz. Se desvanecía la coruja por una esquina, con negro revuelo. Y por donde LA BRUJA se ha ocultado aparece el sorche repatriado. Entra en el claro de luna, la manta terciada, el gorro ladeado, una tagarnina atravesada en los dientes. Recoge la carta. Saluda cuadrándose en la puerta. En los ojos las candelillas de dos copas.

JUANITO VENTOLERA	¿Qué arreglo tenemos, patrón? ¡Como una puñalada ha sido presentarle la boleta! ¿Soy o no soy su alojado, patrón? ¿Qué ha sacado usted del alcalde?
EL BOTICARIO	Dormirás en la cuadra. No tengo mejor acomodo. Mi obligación es procurarte piso y fuego. De ahí no paso. Comes de tu cuenta. Dame esa carta. Me pertenece.
JUANITO VENTOLERA	¿Tiene usted la estafeta en el arroyo?
EL BOTICARIO	La tengo en el forro de los calzones. Dame esa carta.
JUANITO VENTOLERA	Téngala usted.

EL BOTICARIO, con rosma de gato maníaco, se esconde la carta en el bolsillo: Musita rehúso a leerla: Éntrase en la rebotica. La cortineja suspensa de un clavo deja ver la figura soturna y huraña, que tiene una abstracción gesticulante. Cantan dos grillos en el fondo de sus botas nuevas. Lentamente se desnuda del traje dominguero: Se reviste gorro, bata, pantuflas: Reaparece bajo la cortinilla con los ojos parados de través, y toda la cara sobre el mismo lado, torcida con una mueca. La coruja, con esquinado revuelo, ha vuelto a posarse en el iris mágico que abre sus círculos en la acera. El estafermo, gorro y pantuflas, con una espantada, se despega de la cortinilla. El desconcierto de la gambeta y el visaje que le sacude la cara, revierten la vida a una sensación de espejo convexo. La palabra se intuye por el gesto, el golpe de los pies por los ángulos de la zapateta. Es un instante donde todas las cosas se proyectan colmadas de mudez. Se explican plenamente con una angustiosa evidencia visual. La coruja, pegándose al quicio, mete los ojos deslumbrados por la puerta. EL BOTICARIO se dobla como un fantoche.

LA BRUJA	¡Alma de Satanás!
JUANITO VENTOLERA	¡Buena trúpita!

Her voice fades into the distance, and she disappears round a corner with a flapping of her black wings. The veteran squaddie appears around the same corner, materialising in the moonlight. His cloak and cap are lopsided; he has a cheap cigar between his teeth. He picks up the letter. He greets the CHEMIST with a salute. Alcoholic lights dance in his eyes.

JOHNNY BLUSTER	So what's the deal, boss? It's a knife in my own heart, putting you out like this! Can I lodge here or can't I, boss? What did the mayor say?
CHEMIST	You can sleep in the stable. That's the best I can do. I'm obliged to give you a roof over your head and that's all. Meals are your business. Give me that letter. It belongs to me.
JOHNNY BLUSTER	Do you always keep your letters in the gutter?
COURTESAN	No, I keep them where the sun don't shine. Now give me the letter.
JOHNNY BLUSTER	It's yours.

The CHEMIST hisses like a crazed cat; he hides the letter in his pocket, determined not to read it. He mutters under his breath and goes into the back room. His sad, intractable figure, in misanthropic pose, materialises behind a curtain hanging from a nail on the wall. His new boots chirrup like two crickets. Slowly he takes off his best suit and puts on his cap, dressing gown and slippers. He reappears from behind the curtain with his eyes rolled backwards, his whole face twisted into a one-sided rictus. The owl-witch, swooping round the corner, has alighted again in the glare of the magical iris that spills out onto the pavement. The apoplectic CHEMIST, wearing his cap and slippers, suddenly lets go of the curtain in fright. The nervous agitation of his legs and the grimace on his face convey the disconcerting impression that we are viewing the world through a convex mirror. Words are intuited in gestures, the rhythm of his feet in the angular positions of his legs. Muteness reigns: only the anguished visual presence of things can convey what is happening. The owl-witch, hanging onto to the doorframe, thrusts her dazzled gaze across the threshold. The CHEMIST doubles over like a puppet.

WITCH	Christ alive!
JOHNNY BLUSTER	He must be sloshed!

EL GALOPÍN	Es una alferecía que le da por veces.
JUANITO VENTOLERA	¡Cayó fulminado!
EL GALOPÍN	¡Impone mirarle!
JUANITO VENTOLERA	¡Ánimo, patrón!
LA BRUJA	¡Friegas de ortigas por bajo del rabo!

Se anguliza como un murciélago, clavado en los picos del manto: Desaparece en la noche de estrellas. Un gato fugitivo, los ojos en lumbre y el lomo en hopo, en cohete por el canto de la cortinilla, rampa al mostrador, cruza de un salto por encima del fantoche aplastado: Huye con una sardina bajo los bigotes. Viene detrás la vieja, que grita con la escoba enarbolada.

LA BOTICARIA	¡Centellón, que se lleva la cena! ¡Ni el propio enemigo! ¡San Dios, qué retablo! ¡Otra alferecía!
EL GALOPÍN	¡Cayó fulminado!
JUANITO VENTOLERA	Le pasó un aire.
LA BOTICARIA	Hoy se cumple el año. ¡Sócrates, por qué me dejas viuda en este valle de lágrimas!

CALLOW YOUTH	He's prone to fits.
JOHNNY BLUSTER	He's been struck down!
CALLOW YOUTH	Just look at him!
JOHNNY BLUSTER	Come on, boss!
WITCH	I prescribe a good stinging-nettle rub to the groin!

The WITCH angles her arms like a bat's wings; grasping the edges of her cloak, she disappears into the starlit night. A fugitive cat, its eyes ablaze and its hackles raised, shoots like a rocket from behind the curtain, jumps onto the counter, leaps over the crumpled figure of the puppet, and flees with a sardine under its whiskers. The CHEMIST's wife comes after it, yelling, a broom held aloft.

CHEMIST'S WIFE	Damn that cat, it's got our dinner! I wouldn't wish that animal on my worst enemy! Good God, what's this little melodrama? Another fit!
CALLOW YOUTH	He was struck down!
JOHNNY BLUSTER	He's had a funny turn.
CHEMIST'S WIFE	It's been a whole year. Oh Socrates, why have you left me in this vale of tears?

ESCENA TERCERA

Tres pistolos famélicos, con ojos de fiebre, merodean por las eras. PEDRO
MASIDE *camina con dos palomos ocultos en el pecho.* EL BIZCO MALUENDA
esconde los pepinos y tomates para un gazpacho. FRANCO RICOTE, *anda
escotero. Llegan a las tapias del camposanto. Grillos nocturnos. Cruces
y cipreses. Pisa las tumbas un bulto de hombre, que por tiempos se rasca
la nalga, y saca luz en la punta de los dedos para leer los epitafios. Vaga
en un misterio de grillos y luceros.*

PEDRO MASIDE	¡Tenemos a la vista un desertor del Purgatorio! Será conveniente echarle el alto.
EL BIZCO MALUENDA	Parece que el difunto busca el alojamiento y no da con la puerta.
FRANCO RICOTE	¡Alto, amigo! ¡Toda la compañía está roncando, amigo! ¡Se te ha pasado el toque de retreta, a lo que veo!
EL BIZCO MALUENDA	¿Sales de la cantina? ¡Buena hembra es la Iñasi!
FRANCO RICOTE	A lo que parece te gustan las gachís. ¿Por qué no respondes? ¿Te ha comido alguna niña la lengua? No más te hagas el muerto, pues yo te conozco, y sin que hables, he descubierto quién eres. Te diré más: El hallarte aquí es por haber venido acompañando al entierro de tu patrón. Sirves en la Segunda Compañía de Lucena.
EL BIZCO MALUENDA	Escota y vente a cenar. Hay dos palomos y un gazpacho.

*El bulto remoto entre cruces y cipreses, se alumbra rascándose la nalga.
La voz se hace desconocida en los ecos tumbales.*

JUANITO VENTOLERA	Parece que representáis el Juan Tenorio. Pero allí los muertos van a cenar de gorra.

SCENE THREE

Three famished infantrymen with febrile eyes are prowling through some vegetable plots. GALICIAN PEDRO has two pigeons hidden in his jacket. The CROSS-EYED ARAGONESE is hiding enough cucumbers and tomatoes for a gazpacho. FRANCO THE SOUTHERNER is empty handed. They arrive at the wall of the graveyard. Crosses and cypress trees. The bulky shape of a man is walking over the graves; now and again he scratches his backside. His fingertips light up as he strikes a match by which to read the epitaphs. He wanders in a mysterious haze of crickets and stars.

GALICIAN PEDRO	What have we here? A deserter from Purgatory? It's our duty to stop him!
CROSS-EYED ARAGONESE	Maybe he's dead but too hammered to find his resting place!
FRANCO THE SOUTHERNER	Stop there, my friend! The rest of the company has gone to bed! Didn't you hear them sound the curfew?
ARAGONESE	Have you come from the bar? Did you see the bits on that bird?
FRANCO	You do like girls, don't you? Come on, say something! Don't tell me an alleycat's got your tongue. You can stop pretending to be dead, because I know you, even if you won't speak. I recognise you. You came for your landlord's burial. You're in the Second Company of Lucena.
ARAGONESE	If you pay your share you can come and eat: there are two pigeons and a gazpacho.

The distant bulk of the man is lit up between the crosses and the cypress trees as he scratches his backside. His voice is distorted by the echoes of the graveyard.

JOHNNY BLUSTER	I must have stumbled into a performance of Don Juan. But if I had you'd be feeding the dead for free.

FRANCO RICOTE	Convidado quedas. No hemos de ser menos rumbosos que en el teatro.
JUANITO VENTOLERA	¿Dónde es la cita?
FRANCO RICOTE	¡Bien conocido! A la vuelta del Mercado Viejo. Donde dicen Casa de la Sotera.
JUANITO VENTOLERA	No faltaré.
FRANCO RICOTE	¿Aún te quedas?
JUANITO VENTOLERA	El patrón me ha guiñado el ojo al despedirse, y estoy en que algo tiene que contarme. Le había caído simpático, y pudiera en su última voluntad acordarme alguna manda.
FRANCO RICOTE	¡Pues habrá que celebrarlo!
EL BIZCO MALUENDA	¿El difunto tiene aviso de que lo buscas?
JUANITO VENTOLERA	Voy a pasárselo. Justamente aquí está enterrado. Patrón, vamos a vernos las caras. Vengo por la manda que usted me ha dejado.
FRANCO RICOTE	¡Las burlas con los muertos por veces salen caras!
PEDRO MASIDE	¡No apruebo lo que haces!
EL BIZCO MALUENDA	Si un difunto se levanta, la valentía de nada vale. ¿Qué haces en riña con un difunto? ¿Volver a matarlo? Ya está muerto. Si ahora se levantase el boticario, por muchos viajes que le tirásemos puestos los cuatro en rueda, le veríamos siempre derecho.
JUANITO VENTOLERA	¡Eso supuesto que se levantase!
FRANCO RICOTE	Vamos, amigo, deja esa burla y vente a cenar.
JUANITO VENTOLERA	Luego que recoja la manda.
PEDRO MASIDE	¡Ya pasa de desvarío!
EL BIZCO MALUENDA	Ese atolondramiento no lo tuvo ni el propio Juan Tenorio.
PEDRO MASIDE	Ya estás viendo que el muerto no sale de la sepultura. ¡Déjalo en paz!
JUANITO VENTOLERA	Le pesa la losa y hay que ayudarle. ¿Por qué no os llegáis para echar una mano? ¡Vamos a ello, amigos!
EL BIZCO MALUENDA	¡De locura pasa!

FRANCO	Well in the absence of a stone guest you can join us... this may not be the theatre but we can still put our hands in our pockets.[13]
JOHNNY BLUSTER	Where are you headed?
FRANCO	You'll know the place! It's just behind the old market. They call it the *Casa de la Sotera*.
JOHNNY BLUSTER	I'll see you there.
FRANCO	Aren't you coming?
JOHNNY BLUSTER	The boss winked at me just before he croaked. I believe he had something to tell me. He held me in very high regard! In his final moments he might have remembered to leave me a little something.
FRANCO	This calls for a celebration!
ARAGONESE	Does the stiff know you're looking for him?
JOHNNY BLUSTER	He'll find out soon enough. Ah, this is where he's buried. We'll be face-to-face once more, boss! I'm coming for my legacy.
FRANCO	It's a dangerous game, interfering with the dead!
GALICIAN PEDRO	I want nothing to do with it!
ARAGONESE	If you rouse a dead man, it's no good being brave. What can you do against a dead man? You can't kill him: he's already dead. If he rises up now we can stab him as many times as we like and he'll just come back for more.
JOHNNY BLUSTER	That's supposing he rises up!
FRANCO	Come on, my friend, leave it now and come and eat.
JOHNNY BLUSTER	When I've got my legacy.
GALICIAN PEDRO	You must be crazy!
ARAGONESE	Not even Don Juan worked this fast!
GALICIAN PEDRO	Look, he's staying put. Now leave him in peace!
JOHNNY BLUSTER	He can't bear the weight of the tombstone! We've got to help him! Come on, lend me a hand! All together now, friends, heave-ho!
ARAGONESE	He's touched!

PEDRO MASIDE	¡Mucho has pimplado!
FRANCO RICOTE	¡No se levanten a una todos los difuntos y nos puedan!
JUANITO VENTOLERA	Para recoger la manda del patrón, me es preciso dejarle en cueros.
PEDRO MASIDE	¡Mira lo que intentas!
JUANITO VENTOLERA	A eso he venido. ¿Quiere alguno ayudarme?
PEDRO MASIDE	¡Te digo ahora lo que antes te dije! ¡No hay burlas con los muertos!
JUANITO VENTOLERA	¡Ni el caso es de burlas!
EL BIZCO MALUENDA	¡Ahí es nada!
JUANITO VENTOLERA	¡Nada!
EL BIZCO MALUENDA	¡Gachó!
FRANCO RICOTE	Cuando a tanto te pones, conjeturo que con prendas de mucho valor enterraron al difunto.
JUANITO VENTOLERA	¡Un terno de primera! ¡Poco paquete voy a ponerme! Flux completo, como dicen los habaneros.
EL BIZCO MALUENDA	¡Qué va! No será sólo eso.
JUANITO VENTOLERA	Sólo eso. Esta noche tengo que sacar de ganchete a una furcia, y no quiero deslucir a su lado.
FRANCO RICOTE	Camélala que apoquine y te pague un terno de gala.
JUANITO VENTOLERA	Todo se andará, con la ceguera que me muestra.
PEDRO MASIDE	¡La ocurrencia de vestirte la ropa del difunto te la sopló el Diablo!
JUANITO VENTOLERA	¿Tan mala os parece?
PEDRO MASIDE	Tiene dos caras esa moneda.
EL BIZCO MALUENDA	La ocurrencia no es para despreciarla. Ahora que se requiere un corazón muy intrépido.
JUANITO VENTOLERA	Yo lo tengo.
FRANCO RICOTE	Si te falta, se te viene encima todo el batallón de los muertos.
JUANITO VENTOLERA	No me faltará.
FRANCO RICOTE	Me alegraré.

GALICIAN PEDRO	He's tanked!
FRANCO	What if the dead rise up? What if they overpower us?
JOHNNY BLUSTER	If I'm going to get my legacy, I've got to strip him.
GALICIAN PEDRO	Strip him!
JOHNNY BLUSTER	That's what I said. Isn't anyone going to help me?
GALICIAN PEDRO	I've said it before and I'll say it again: interfering with the dead is a dangerous game!
JOHNNY BLUSTER	It's not a game!
ARAGONESE	Who said anything about games?
JOHNNY BLUSTER	Games have got nothing to do with it.
ARAGONESE	Christ!
FRANCO	I presume they buried the dead man in his finery, since you're going to so much trouble.
JOHNNY BLUSTER	In a top-notch whistle! I'll look a dandy, all decked out from head to foot.
ARAGONESE	Come off it! You must be after more than just a suit!
JOHNNY BLUSTER	The suit and nothing but the suit. Tonight I'm fixed up with a lovely whore, and I want to be looking my best.
FRANCO	So warm her up and get her to dish out for a new suit.
JOHNNY BLUSTER	I'm all a-quiver, gents... she's got quite a soft spot for me!
GALICIAN PEDRO	Stealing a dead man's clothes… that's the devil talking.
JOHNNY BLUSTER	Oh come on, it's not that bad!
GALICIAN PEDRO	There's another side to this coin! It could flip either way!
ARAGONESE	As ideas go it's not to be sneezed at, though it's not for the faint hearted.
JOHNNY BLUSTER	Who's faint hearted?
FRANCO	You'd be fighting off a battalion of the dead if you were.
JOHNNY BLUSTER	I'm not.
FRANCO	Just as well.

JUANITO VENTOLERA	¿Ninguno quiere darme su ayuda?
EL BIZCO MALUENDA	Me parece que ninguno.
PEDRO MASIDE	Yo, por mi parte, no. Para pelear con hombres, cuenta conmigo, pero no para despojar muertos.
JUANITO VENTOLERA	¿Pues qué otra cosa se hacía en campaña?
PEDRO MASIDE	No es lo mismo.
FRANCO RICOTE	Claramente que no. En un camposanto la sepultura es tierra sagrada.
JUANITO VENTOLERA	¡No se me había ocurrido este escrúpulo!
EL BIZCO MALUENDA	¡Que salgas avante!
FRANCO RICOTE	Tienes plato en la cena.

JOHNNY BLUSTER	Isn't anyone going to help me?
ARAGONESE	Doesn't look like it.
GALICIAN PEDRO	You can count me out. I'll fight the living, but you won't catch me robbing the dead.
JOHNNY BLUSTER	What was it we were doing in Cuba then?
GALICIAN PEDRO	That was different.
FRANCO	Of course it was. In a graveyard tombs are sacred.
JOHNNY BLUSTER	What fine scruples! I hadn't thought of that.
ARAGONESE	Good luck to you.
FRANCO	Come and eat when you're ready.

ESCENA CUARTA

Casa de la Sotera: Huerto con emparrados. Luna y luceros, bajo los palios de la vid, conciertan penumbras moradas y verdosas. A la vera alba del pozo, fragante entre arriates de albahaca, está puesta una mesa con manteles. La camarada de los tres pistolos mata la espera con el vino chispón de aquel pago, y decora el triple gesto palurdo con perfiles flamencos.

PEDRO MASIDE	¡Ese punto, no más parece. Filo de las doce tenemos. ¿Qué se hace?
EL BIZCO MALUENDA	Pedir la cena.
FRANCO RICOTE	Esperémosle un rato por si llega. Estaría divertido que el difunto se lo hubiese llevado de las orejas al Infierno.
EL BIZCO MALUENDA	¡Vaya un barbián!
FRANCO RICOTE	¿Tú de qué le conoces, Maside?
PEDRO MASIDE	Somos de pueblos vecinos.
EL BIZCO MALUENDA	¿Gallego es ese sujeto? No lo aparenta.
PEDRO MASIDE	¿Y por qué no? Galicia da hombres tan buenos como la mejor tierra.
EL BIZCO MALUENDA	Para cargar fardos.
PEDRO MASIDE	No sabes ni la media. Y con ese hablar descubres que tan siquiera estás al tanto de lo que ponen los papeles. ¿Tú has visto retratado el Ministerio? Este amigo que calla, lo ha visto y dirá si no vienen allí puestos cuatro gallegos.
EL BIZCO MALUENDA	¡Ladrones de la política!
PEDRO MASIDE	¡Tampoco te contradigo! Pero muy agudos y de mucho provecho.
EL BIZCO MALUENDA	Para sus casas!
PEDRO MASIDE	Para ministros del Rey.
EL BIZCO MALUENDA	¿Vas con eso a significar que sois los primeros?
PEDRO MASIDE	¡Tampoco somos los últimos!
FRANCO RICOTE	La tierra más pelada puede dar hombres de mérito, amigos.
EL BIZCO MALUENDA	¡Gachó! ¡Tú has dicho la mejor sentencia!

SCENE FOUR

The Casa de la Sotera: a garden shaded with vines. The moon and stars cast purple shadows beneath the green canopy. At the white edge of a pond, fragrant between beds of sweet basil, is a table laid with a cloth. The three infantrymen are grouped together, killing time and drinking the frisky local wine. Their flamenco profiles lend a decorative quality to their triple coarseness.

GALICIAN PEDRO	He's not coming. It's nearly midnight. What shall we do?
ARAGONESE	Let's eat.
FRANCO	No, wait a bit longer, he might still come. Or maybe the stiff's carried him off to hell by the ears! What a laugh!
ARAGONESE	Charming!
FRANCO	How do you know him, Pedro?
GALICIAN PEDRO	We're from neighbouring towns.
ARAGONESE	Is he from Galicia? I wouldn't have guessed it.
GALICIAN PEDRO	Why not? Galicia's as good as anywhere.
ARAGONESE	For breeding packhorses.
GALICIAN PEDRO	What would you know? You obviously haven't been reading the papers lately. Have you seen that picture of the new government? Our southern friend here, who's keeping quiet for some reason, has seen it and he'll tell you there are four Galicians in it.
ARAGONESE	Nothing but thieves in politicians' clothing!
GALICIAN PEDRO	I don't disagree! But very bright and valuable!
ARAGONESE	To themselves!
GALICIAN PEDRO	No, to the King's government.
ARAGONESE	Do you mean to say you're the best?
GALICIAN PEDRO	We're not the worst!
FRANCO	The most barren land can produce good men, my friends.
ARAGONESE	You're not wrong! You've hit the nail on the head!

FRANCO RICOTE	Pues me beberé el chato del pelmazo que nos tiene enredados en la espera.
EL BIZCO MALUENDA	¡Y que se retarda!
PEDRO MASIDE	¡Si los difuntos se levantaron en batallón, ha de verse negro para salir del camposanto!
EL BIZCO MALUENDA	¡Ese toque de llamada se queda para el día del Juicio Final!
PEDRO MASIDE	¡Como le hagan la rueda, no se verá libre hasta la del alba! Cuantos han pasado por ello, tienen dicho haber peleado toda la noche, y que los muertos caían y se levantaban.
FRANCO RICOTE	Ello está claro. A los muertos no se les mata.
EL BIZCO MALUENDA	No creo una palabra de tales peteneras.
PEDRO MASIDE	¡La creencia no se enseña!
EL BIZCO MALUENDA	¡Que se pronuncien los difuntos me parece una pura camama! ¡Para tus luces, este mundo y el otro bailan en pareja!
PEDRO MASIDE	Hay correspondencia.
EL BIZCO MALUENDA	¿Y batallones sublevados?
PEDRO MASIDE	Estoy pelado al cero.
EL BIZCO MALUENDA	¿Y Capitanes Generales descontentos?
PEDRO MASIDE	Vamos a dejarlo.
EL BIZCO MALUENDA	¡Panoli! ¡En el otro mundo no se reconocen los grados!
PEDRO MASIDE	Poco se me da de tu pitorreo.

Aparece JUANITO VENTOLERA, transfigurado con las galas del difunto. Camisa planchada, terno negro, botas nuevas con canto de grillos. Ninguna cobertura en la cabeza: Bajo la luna, tiene un halo verdoso.

JUANITO VENTOLERA	¡Salud, amigos! Hay que dispensar el retardo.
EL BIZCO MALUENDA	A tiempo llegas.
PEDRO MASIDE	Ya estábamos con algún recelo.
FRANCO RICOTE	Te habíamos sospechado de orejas en el Infierno.
EL BIZCO MALUENDA	Y alguno, con el batallón de muertos a la rueda de pan y canela.

FRANCO	Well I'm sick of waiting for this prune and I'm drinking his wine.
ARAGONESE	What's taking him so long?
GALICIAN PEDRO	If the dead all rise up together, I don't fancy his chances of getting out of the graveyard!
ARAGONESE	The bells will toll for the final day of judgement!
GALICIAN PEDRO	If they surround him, he won't get away until the bells ring for morning mass! I've heard others say they fought all night, but the dead just kept falling and getting up again.
FRANCO	That's for sure. You can't kill a corpse.
ARAGONESE	I don't believe a word of all this rubbish.
GALICIAN PEDRO	Some people have no faith.
ARAGONESE	Are the dead having a little rebellion of their own? Don't tell me: this world and the next dance cheek to cheek.
GALICIAN PEDRO	They correspond.
ARAGONESE	Do the dead have mutinous battalions?
GALICIAN PEDRO	I'm skint.
ARAGONESE	And discontented Generals?
GALICIAN PEDRO	Let's drop it.
ARAGONESE	Grow up! The spirit world isn't organised by military rank.
GALICIAN PEDRO	You can make fun all you like.

JOHNNY BLUSTER appears, transfigured by the dead man's clothes. An ironed shirt, a black suit, new boots that chirrup like crickets. His head is bare; the moonlight gives him a greenish halo.

JOHNNY BLUSTER	Good evening, friends, countrymen! Pray forgive my late arrival.
ARAGONESE	It's about time you got here.
GALICIAN PEDRO	We were starting to wonder what had happened to you.
FRANCO	We thought you'd been dragged off to hell by the ears.
ARAGONESE	And one of our company thought you'd been playing ring a ring o' roses with a battalion of the dead.

JUANITO VENTOLERA	Ése ha sido mi paisano Pedro Maside.
PEDRO MASIDE	Justamente. Tú habrás librado sin contratiempo, pero ello no desmiente lo que otros cuentan.
JUANITO VENTOLERA	¿No me oléis a chamusco? He visitado las calderas del rancho que atiza Pedro Botero.
EL BIZCO MALUENDA	¿Y lo has probado?
JUANITO VENTOLERA	Y me ha sabido a maná. En el cuartel lo quisiéramos.
EL BIZCO MALUENDA	Bébete un chato, y cuenta por derecho! ¿El vestido que traes es la propia mortaja del fiambre?
JUANITO VENTOLERA	¡La propia!
FRANCO RICOTE	¿Lo has dejado en cueros?
JUANITO VENTOLERA	Le propuse la changa con mi rayadillo, y no se mostró contrario.
EL BIZCO MALUENDA	Visto lo cual, habéis changado.
JUANITO VENTOLERA	Veo que lo entiendes.
EL BIZCO MALUENDA	El terno es fino.
JUANITO VENTOLERA	De primera.
EL BIZCO MALUENDA	Y te va a la medida. Sólo te falta un bombín para ser un pollo petenera. El patrón se lo habrá olvidado en la percha, y debes reclamárselo a la viuda.
JUANITO VENTOLERA	Me das una idea...
EL BIZCO MALUENDA	¿Tendrías redaños?
JUANITO VENTOLERA	Aventúrate unas copas.
PEDRO MASIDE	¡Sobrepasaba el escarnio!
FRANCO RICOTE	¡Ni el tan mentado Juan Tenorio! ¡Y tú, gachó, no hables en verso!
EL BIZCO MALUENDA	Te aventuro los cuatro cafeses.
JUANITO VENTOLERA	¡Van! ¿Y vosotros no queréis jugaros la copa?
FRANCO RICOTE	¿Tú te la juegas?
JUANITO VENTOLERA	¡Dicho está!
EL BIZCO MALUENDA	¡Gachó! ¡Te hago la apuesta aun cuando me toque ser paduano! Vamos a ver hasta dónde llega tu rejo.

JOHNNY BLUSTER	My compatriot Pedro, no doubt.
GALICIAN PEDRO	You're not wrong. You might have escaped unscathed, but that doesn't give the lie to the rest.
JOHNNY BLUSTER	Can you smell the sulphur on me? I've been stirring boiling cauldrons with Lucifer.
ARAGONESE	And did you taste what was in them?
JOHNNY BLUSTER	Yes, and it was like manna from heaven. It was better than the food we got in the barracks.
ARAGONESE	Knock one back and tell us straight! Is that really the corpse's clobber?
JOHNNY BLUSTER	The very same.
FRANCO	Did you leave him in his birthday suit?
JOHNNY BLUSTER	I exchanged his outfit for my nice striped uniform. I think it was a fair swap! He didn't seem to mind at least.
ARAGONESE	I bet he thought it was a steal.
JOHNNY BLUSTER	I see you're with me on this one.
ARAGONESE	The material's very fine.
JOHNNY BLUSTER	It's top drawer.
ARAGONESE	It fits you like a dream. You just need a bowler hat and you could strut with the best of them! I bet the boss left it on the stand: why don't you go and ask his widow for it?
JOHNNY BLUSTER	Now that's an idea…
ARAGONESE	You wouldn't dare!
JOHNNY BLUSTER	How many drinks are in it?
GALICIAN PEDRO	That's really pushing it!
FRANCO	Not even Don Juan would go that far! Now listen, don't you start reciting verse at me…!
ARAGONESE	A cup of coffee each!
JOHNNY BLUSTER	Done! How about the rest of you, will you stake a drink on it?
FRANCO	Will you?
JOHNNY BLUSTER	Why not?
ARAGONESE	Christ! I don't even care if I lose! I just want to see what lengths you'll go to.

JUANITO VENTOLERA La visita a la viuda no pasa de ser un cumplimiento.

EL BIZCO MALUENDA ¿Qué plazo le pones?

JUANITO VENTOLERA Esta noche, después de la cena. ¿Tú no apuestas nada, paisano Maside? ¿Temes perder?

PEDRO MASIDE Tengo conciencia, y no quiero animarte por el camino que llevas.

JUANITO VENTOLERA ¿Tan malo te parece, paisano?

PEDRO MASIDE De perdición completa.

JUANITO VENTOLERA Dando la cara no hay bueno ni malo.

PEDRO MASIDE Para vivir seguro, fuera de ley, se requieren muchos parneses. Das la cara, y te sepultan en presidio.

FRANCO RICOTE O te tullen para toda la vida con un solfeo.

JUANITO VENTOLERA ¡Hay que ser soberbio y dar la cara contra el mundo entero! A mí me cae simpático el Diablo.

PEDRO MASIDE Con dar la cara no acallas la conciencia.

JUANITO VENTOLERA Yo respondo de todas mis acciones, y con esto sólo, ninguno me iguala. El hombre que no se pone fuera de la ley, es un cabra.

EL BIZCO MALUENDA Con otros chatos lo discutiremos.

JOHNNY BLUSTER	It's only polite to call in on the widow.
ARAGONESE	When will you do the deed?
JOHNNY BLUSTER	Tonight, after I've eaten. How about you Pedro, my compatriot? Aren't you going to have a flutter? Scared you'll lose?
GALICIAN PEDRO	I have a conscience, and it's telling me not to push you any further down this road.
JOHNNY BLUSTER	Where's the harm in it, friend?
GALICIAN PEDRO	It's a mortal sin.
JOHNNY BLUSTER	I'm just standing up for myself. There's no right or wrong in that.
GALICIAN PEDRO	If you want to live safely outside the law, you need plenty of scratch.Stand up for yourself and they'll bury you alive in prison.
FRANCO	Or cripple you with the whip for the rest of your life.
JOHNNY BLUSTER	The important thing is to stand proud and face the world head on! With the devil for company.
GALICIAN PEDRO	Standing proud won't quiet your conscience.
JOHNNY BLUSTER	I take responsibility for all my actions, and that raises me above the ordinary man! Men who live inside the law are no better than sheep.
ARAGONESE	Let's chat about it over another glass of plink-plonk.

ESCENA QUINTA

La botica, con dos sombras en la acera, sobre las luces mágicas del ojo nigromante. Dentro, la viuda enlutada, con parches en las sienes, hace ganchillo tras el mostrador. Maja el GALOPÍN en el gran mortero. El SACRISTÁN y el RAPISTA, aparejados, saludan en la puerta.

EL RAPISTA	Está muy solitaria, Doña Terita. Las amigas debieran hacer más por acompañarla en estas tristes circunstancias.
LA BOTICARIA	Y no me falta su consuelo. Ahora se fueron las de enfrente.
EL SACRISTÁN	Visto como usted se había quedado tan sola, hemos entrado.
LA BOTICARIA	Pasen ustedes. ¡Niño, deja esa matraca, que me quiebras la cabeza!
EL RAPISTA	Doña Terita, usted siempre a la labor de ganchillo, sobreponiéndose a su acerba pena.
LA BOTICARIA	Crea usted que me distrae. Niño, echa los cierres.
EL SACRISTÁN	Da usted ejemplo a muchas vecinas.
LA BOTICARIA	No faltará quien me moteje.
EL SACRISTÁN	¡Qué reputación no muerde la envidia, mi señora Doña Terita!
EL RAPISTA	¡Y en esta vecindad!
EL SACRISTÁN	Por donde usted vaya verá los mismos ejemplos, Doña Terita. Toda la España es una demagogia. Esta disolución viene de la Prensa.
EL RAPISTA	Ahora le han puesto mordaza.
EL SACRISTÁN	Cuando el mal no tiene cura.
EL RAPISTA	¡Y tampoco es unánime en el escalpelo toda la Prensa! La hay mala y la hay buena. Vean ustedes publicaciones como *Blanco y Negro*. Doña Terita, si usted desea distraerse algún rato, disponga usted de la colección completa. Es la vanagloria que tiene un servidor y el ornato de su establecimiento.

SCENE FIVE

The chemist's. On the pavement, two shadows have been cast over the magical lights of the necromancer's eye. Inside, dressed in mourning and with a compress on each temple, the widow is crocheting behind the counter. The CALLOW YOUTH is grinding something in a large mortar. The SEXTON and the BARBER are paired in the doorway, greeting the widow.

BARBER	We're sorry to see you alone, Doña Terita. Your friends should do more to keep you company at this sad time.
CHEMIST'S WIFE	They've been very kind to me. My neighbours were here a while ago.
SEXTON	When we saw you were alone, we thought we'd come and see you.
CHEMIST'S WIFE	Come in. Stop pounding will you, boy, I've got a splitting headache!
BARBER	Doña Terita, here you are crocheting, refusing to give in to your pain.
CHEMIST'S WIFE	It helps take my mind off it. Lock up would you, boy?
SEXTON	You're a good example to the other women.
CHEMIST'S WIFE	I'm sure they'll be calling me names.
SEXTON	Envy always snaps at the heels of goodness I'm afraid, my dear Doña Terita!
BARBER	Especially around here!
SEXTON	It's the same everywhere, Doña Terita. Spain is the land of the demagogues! If the nation is dissolute, I blame the press!
BARBER	The press has been gagged.
SEXTON	Tough times call for tough measures!
BARBER	But not all the press wields the scalpel in the same way! Some publications are better than others! Take a nice illustrated magazine like *Blanco y Negro*.[14] Doña Terita, if you want to take your mind off things for a while, I can humbly offer you every one of its past issues. They are my pride and joy and the jewel in my establishment's crown.

| LA BOTICARIA | Creo que trae muy buenas cosas esa publicación. |
| EL RAPISTA | ¡De todo! Retratos de las celebridades más célebres. La Familia Real, Machaquito, La Imperio. ¡El célebre toro Coronel! ¡El fenómeno más grande de las plazas españolas, que tomó quince varas y mató once caballos! En bodas y bautizos publica fotografías de lo mejor. Un emporio de recetas: ¡Allí, culinarias! ¡Allí, composturas para toda clase de vidrios y porcelanas! ¡Allí, licorería! ¡Allí, quitamanchas!... |

EL RAPISTA, menudo, petulante, apologético, cachea en la petaca, sopla las hojas de un librillo, y una que arranca se la pega en el labio. EL SACRISTÁN, con aire cazurro, por las sisas de la sotana se registraba los calzones: Saca, envuelto en un pañuelo de yerbas, el cuaderno de la Cofradía del Santo Sepulcro: Con la uña anota una página y se la muestra a la viuda, que suspira, puestos los lentes en la punta de la nariz.

EL SACRISTÁN	¡Doña Terita, si no le sirve de molestia, quiere usted pasar la vista por esta anotación y firmar en ella su conforme? ¡Siempre en el supuesto de que no le sirva de molestia!
LA BOTICARIA	¡Pero aquí, qué pones?
EL SACRISTÁN	El pico del entierro.
LA BOTICARIA	¡Pero tú tienes conciencia?
EL SACRISTÁN	Me parece.
LA BOTICARIA	¡Esta cuenta es un sacrilegio!
EL SACRISTÁN	Doña Terita, es usted la mar de célebre.
LA BOTICARIA	¡Un robo escandaloso! ¡Siete duros de cera!
EL SACRISTÁN	Y aún pierde siete reales la iglesia. La cera consumida sube ese pico. Siete reales que pierde la iglesia.
LA BOTICARIA	¡El armonio cinco duros! ¡Pero cuándo se ha visto?

CHEMIST'S WIFE	I believe it's full of very interesting things.
BARBER	Oh, very! It has pictures of the most famous celebrities. The royal family; the most daring bullfighters; the stars of our theatrical firmament. Even *Coronel*, the bull they're calling the most amazing phenomenon of Spain's bullrings! He took fifteen pikes and killed eleven horses! They print the loveliest photos of weddings and christenings. And there's a veritable emporium of useful recipes! Dear lady, do you seek information about cookery? It's there! Craftwork? It's there! Home brewing? It's there! Stain removal? It's there!

The BARBER – short, petulant, and apologetic – rummages in a cigarette case. He pulls out a booklet of rolling papers, riffles them with his breath, then tears one off and sticks it to his lip. The SEXTON, looking sullen, feels around in his underwear through the armholes of his cassock. He pulls out a notebook, wrapped in a brightly checked handkerchief: it is the account book of the Brotherhood of the Holy Sepulchre. He lays a fingernail on one of its pages and shows it to the widow, who sighs, balancing her glasses on the end of her nose.

SEXTON	If it's not too much trouble, Doña Terita, could you cast your eye over this entry and sign it? If it's not too much trouble, of course!
CHEMIST'S WIFE	What's this?
SEXTON	It's the bill for your husband's burial.
CHEMIST'S WIFE	Have you no shame?
SEXTON	What have I said?
CHEMIST'S WIFE	This is sacrilege!
SEXTON	Doña Terita, you are very well known in the town.
CHEMIST'S WIFE	It's scandalous; it's daylight robbery! Seven *duros* for wax candles!
SEXTON	And even so the church is losing out on seven *reales*. We used more wax than the price indicates. That's seven *reales* the church is losing out on!
CHEMIST'S WIFE	Five *duros* for the organist! It's unheard of!

EL SACRISTÁN	El armonio y dos cantores. ¡Es la tarifa!
LA BOTICARIA	¡Con estos precios ahuyentáis la fe! ¡Las misas a once reales es un escándalo! ¡Pero adónde me van a subir las misas Gregorianas?...
EL SACRISTÁN	¡Y la rebaja de pena que usted puede llevar con esos sufragios al finado! ¡Todo hay que ponerlo en balanza, Doña Terita!
LA BOTICARIA	Las indulgencias no debían cobrarse.
EL SACRISTÁN	¡Sin eso, a morir! ¡Usted considere que no tiene otras aduanas la Santa Madre Iglesia!
EL RAPISTA	Opino como Doña Terita. La Iglesia debía operar con mayor economía. No digamos de balde, pero casamientos, bautizos y sepelios están sobrecargados en un cincuenta por ciento.
LA BOTICARIA	¡Y eso no se llama usura!
EL SACRISTÁN	¡Que va usted degenerando en herética, Doña Terita!
LA BOTICARIA	¡Pues vele con el cuento al Nuncio Apostólico!
EL SACRISTÁN	Usted está nerviosa.
LA BOTICARIA	¡Cómo no estarlo!
EL RAPISTA	Doña Terita, visto el mal resultado de este amigo, yo me najo sin presentar mi factura.
LA BOTICARIA	Puede usted hacerlo.
EL RAPISTA	¿No será demasiada jaqueca?
la BOTICARIA	¡Ya que estoy en ello!... Niño, apaga los globos de la puerta.

EL RAPISTA, con destreza de novillero, salta por encima del mostrador: Finústico y petulante, le presenta el papel a la viuda, que lo repasa alzándose los lentes, sin cabalgarlos: Gesto desdeñoso y resignado de pulcra Artemisa Boticaria.

EL RAPISTA	Doña Terita, si le parece dejarlo para otra ocasión, no se hable más, y a sus órdenes.
LA BOTICARIA	Liquidaremos ahora. ¿Qué ha puesto usted aquí? ¡Una peseta!

SEXTON	The organist and two choristers. That's what it costs!
CHEMIST'S WIFE	If you charge people these prices they'll become atheists! Eleven *reales* for a mass! It's scandalous! What on earth do you charge for the Gregorian masses?
SEXTON	But just think how you are smoothing your beloved husband's way to heaven! It will considerably ease your pain, my dear lady! It must all be weighed and balanced!
CHEMIST'S WIFE	You can't charge for absolution!
SEXTON	How would we manage if we didn't? What other levies can the Holy Mother Church impose?
BARBER	I agree with Doña Terita. The church should be more economical. You can't work for nothing, of course, but you overcharge for weddings, baptisms and funerals by fifty percent!
CHEMIST'S WIFE	And if that's not usury I don't know what is!
SEXTON	Doña Terita, you are turning into a heretic!
CHEMIST'S WIFE	Run and tell it to the Pope!
SEXTON	Your nerves have got the better of you.
CHEMIST'S WIFE	Is it any wonder?
BARBER	Doña Terita, in light of your disagreement with our friend here, I will simply tear up my bill.
CHEMIST'S WIFE	No, come on, let's see it.
BARBER	I would hate this to be a headache for you!
CHEMIST'S WIFE	Too late, it is already! Turn out the lamps above the door would you, boy?

Nimble as a bullfighter's apprentice, the BARBER leaps over the counter and, with obsequious petulance, presents the widow with his bill. She looks down her nose at it, holding her glasses primly aloft with the resigned disdain of a chemist's-shop Artemis.

BARBER	Doña Terita, if you would rather leave it for another occasion, we won't talk about it again, and I am your humble servant.
CHEMIST'S WIFE	No, let's sort it out now. What have you written

EL RAPISTA	Pastilla jabón d'olor, para adecentamiento del finado.
LA BOTICARIA	¿Y esta partida?
EL RAPISTA	De hacerle la barba.
LA BOTICARIA	Mi finado tenía con usted un arreglo.
EL RAPISTA	¡Doña Terita, esa partida está rebajada en un cincuenta por ciento! Yo le hago la barba a un viviente por tres perras, pero usted no se representa lo que impone un muerto enjabonado. ¡Y su esposo no ha sido de los menos! También tenga usted por sabido que las barbas de los muertos son muy resistentes y mellan toda la herramienta.
LA BOTICARIA	¡Dos pesetas es un escándalo!
EL RAPISTA	Pues pone usted aquello que tenga voluntad. Y si no quiere poner nada, borra el cargo de la factura.
LA BOTICARIA	Naturalmente. ¿Quiere usted cobrar ahora?
EL RAPISTA	Si lo tiene por bueno.
LA BOTICARIA	Tres cincuenta. ¡Qué robo más escandaloso!
EL SACRISTÁN	Doña Terita, es usted la mar de célebre.
LA BOTICARIA	Niño, entorna la puerta.
EL SACRISTÁN	Doña Terita, si acuerda que se digan las Gregorianas, sírvase pasar un aviso a la Parroquia. Y no la molesto más, que usted desea retirarse a las sábanas.
EL RAPISTA	Doña Terita, suscribo las palabras del amigo. En su situación de viuda nerviosa, la mejor medicina es el descanso.

La viuda suspira, aprieta la boca, se abstrae en la contemplación de sus manos con mitones. EL GALOPÍN, al canto de la puerta, desdobla media hoja. Se enhebran por la abertura SACRISTÁN y rapabarbas.

	here? One *peseta*!
BARBER	For one bar of fragrant soap, essential to the preparation of the deceased.
CHEMIST'S WIFE	And what is this?
BARBER	Ah, that is for the trimming of the beard.
CHEMIST'S WIFE	My husband had an agreement with you!
BARBER	Doña Terita, I have given you a discount of fifty percent on that particular service! I charge almost nothing to trim the beard of a living man, but you can't imagine how difficult it is to work with a soapy corpse! And your husband was not an easy customer! You should know that a dead man's beard is very coarse, and causes untold damage to a barber's precious tools!
CHEMIST'S WIFE	Two *pesetas*? It's scandalous.
BARBER	Then I beg you pay me what you think is right. And if you prefer to pay nothing at all, just cancel the invoice.
CHEMIST'S WIFE	Oh, of course. Shall I pay you now?
BARBER	If it's no bother.
CHEMIST'S WIFE	Three-fifty. It's daylight robbery!
SEXTON	Doña Terita, you are very well known in the town.
CHEMIST'S WIFE	Open the door for these gentlemen, boy.
SEXTON	Doña Terita, if you decide you would like the Gregorian masses, do let me know. You look tired, dear lady; we'll let you retire to your bed.
BARBER	Doña Terita, let me echo the sentiments of our good friend here. In your widowed state, the surest way to calm your nerves is to rest.

The widow sighs and purses her lips. She loses herself in contemplation of her gloved hands. The CALLOW YOUTH half opens the door, and the SEXTON and the BARBER thread their way through the opening onto the street.

ESCENA SEXTA

En el cielo raso, un globo de luz. Alcoba grande y pulcra, cromos y santicos por las paredes. El tálamo de hierro fundido y boliches de cristal traslúcido, perfila bajo la luz, el costado donde roncaba el difunto. En la pila del agua bendita, un angelote toca el clarinete – alones azules, faldellín movido al viento, las rosadas pantorrillas en un cruce de bolero –. Entra DOÑA TERITA quitándose los postizos del moño: Se detiene en el círculo de luz, con una horquilla atravesada en la boca. Resuena la casa con fuertes aldabonazos. DOÑA TERITA, soltándose las enaguas, retrocede a la puerta.

LA BOTICARIA	Asómate, niño, a la ventana. Mira quién sea. No abras sin bien cerciorarte.
EL GALOPÍN	¡Qué más cercioro! Por el estruendo que mete es el punto alojado.
LA BOTICARIA	Pues no le abras. Que duerma al sereno.
EL GALOPÍN	Es muy capaz de apedrearnos las tejas.
LA BOTICARIA	¡Pues no se le abre! ¡Ese hombre me da miedo!
EL GALOPÍN	¡Tendremos escándalo toda la noche!
LA BOTICARIA	¡Ya se cansará de repicar!
EL GALOPÍN	Viene de la taberna, y el vino es muy temoso.

Cesan los golpes. La casa queda en silencio. Parpadea una mariposa en el globo de luz. LA BOTICARIA y el dependiente, en asustada mudez, alargan la oreja. Alguien ha rozado los hierros del balcón.

EL GALOPÍN	¡Ahí le tenemos!
LA BOTICARIA	¡Jesús, mil veces! ¡Artes de ladrón tiene el malvado!
EL GALOPÍN	Nada se sacó con dejarle fuera!

Saltan con fracaso de cristales, estremecidas, rebotantes, las puertas del balcón. JUANITO VENTOLERA, entre los quicios, algarero y farsante, hace una reverencia.

SCENE SIX

A globe of light shines in the clear sky. A large, clean room, with picture cards and images of saints on the walls, and a wrought-iron double bed with translucent glass bedknobs. The light from outside illuminates the side on which the deceased used to snore. A fat angel is playing the clarinet on a basin of holy water. It has plucked blue wings, underskirts that blow in the breeze, and its pink calves are crossed as if it were dancing the bolero. DOÑA TERITA enters, removing the hairpiece from her bun: she stops in the circle of light, a hairpin between her teeth. The house is filled with the sound of loud knocking. Loosening her petticoats, DOÑA TERITA walks back towards the door.

CHEMIST'S WIFE	Boy, have a look out of the window! Who is it? Don't open up until you are sure.
CALLOW YOUTH	As if I didn't know! Judging by the noise he's making, it's that digger we've got to put up.
CHEMIST'S WIFE	Well don't let him in. He can sleep outside.
CALLOW YOUTH	He might start chucking stones at the roof. I wouldn't put it past him.
CHEMIST'S WIFE	Don't let him in! He frightens me!
CALLOW YOUTH	He'll carry on all night!
CHEMIST'S WIFE	He'll give up eventually.
CALLOW YOUTH	He's come from the bar. He reeks of cheap Dutch courage.

The banging stops. The house goes quiet. A moth flutters in the globe of light. The CHEMIST'S WIFE and the assistant, frightened and mute, lean forward to listen. Something scrapes against the iron bars of the balcony.

CALLOW YOUTH	There he is!
CHEMIST'S WIFE	Oh God, oh God! The reprobate's a thief now!
CALLOW YOUTH	It's no good leaving him outside!

The doors of the balcony crash open with a shattering of glass, swinging and juddering on their hinges. Framed in the doorway, JOHNNY BLUSTER

JUANITO VENTOLERA	Doña Terita, traigo para usted una visita de su finado.
LA BOTICARIA	¡A la falta de respeto une usted el escarnio!
JUANITO VENTOLERA	¡Palabra, Doña Terita! El difunto me ha designado por su albacea, y usted puede comprobar que no digo mentira si se digna concederme una mirada de sus bellos ojos. ¿Teme usted enamorarse, Doña Terita? No lo deje usted por ese miramiento, que tendrá usted por mi parte una fina correspondencia.
LA BOTICARIA	¡Váyase usted, o alboroto la vecindad y la duerme usted en la cárcel!
JUANITO VENTOLERA	Doña Terita, mejor le irá conservándose afónica.

JUANITO VENTOLERA entra en la alcoba, haciendo piernas, mofador y chispón, los brazos en jarra. DOÑA TERITA se desploma perlática: En el círculo de luz queda abierto el ruedo de las faldas. EL GALOPÍN, revolante el mandilón, se acoge a la puerta. DOÑA TERITA se dramatiza con un grito.

LA BOTICARIA	¡Niño, no me dejes!
JUANITO VENTOLERA	¡Doña Terita, usted me ofende con ese recelo! ¡No vea usted en mí al punto alojado! Es una visita del llorado cadáver la que le traigo, téngalo usted presente. Si entro por el balcón, usted lo ha impuesto no queriendo franquearme la puerta.
LA BOTICARIA	Se irá usted a dormir fuera. Yo le pago la posada.

DOÑA TERITA se tuerce sobre el regazo la faltriquera, y cuenta las perronas: Con ellas van saliendo el alfiletero, las llaves, un ovillo de lana.

JUANITO VENTOLERA	Es poco el suelto, Doña Terita.
LA BOTICARIA	¡Dos pesetas! ¡Muy suficiente!
JUANITO VENTOLERA	¡Una pringue! Menda se hospeda en los mejores hoteles. Ya lo discutiremos, si usted se obceca. Sepa usted que el llorado cadáver se ha conducido

makes a stagey and outrageous bow.

JOHNNY BLUSTER	Doña Terita, I bring a message from your dead husband.
CHEMIST'S WIFE	Not only do you have no respect, you're making fun of me too!
JOHNNY BLUSTER	It's true, Doña Terita! I'm your husband's executor! If you want to see for yourself, just grace me with a look from those beautiful eyes! Are you afraid you'll fall in love with me, Doña Terita? Oh, you mustn't be afraid; your love won't be unrequited, I assure you.
CHEMIST'S WIFE	Go away, or I'll wake the whole street and you'll be locked up for the night!
JOHNNY BLUSTER	Doña Terita, things will go better for you if you keep your mouth shut.

JOHNNY BLUSTER saunters tipsily into the room, his hands resting sardonically on his hips. DOÑA TERITA's legs buckle beneath her: her skirts pool around her in the circle of light. The CALLOW YOUTH flaps and cowers by the door. DOÑA TERITA comes to life dramatically with a scream.

CHEMIST'S WIFE	Don't leave me, boy!
JOHNNY BLUSTER	Doña Terita, you're hurting my feelings! Don't think of me as some unwanted lodger! Look, I've brought your dearly departed to see you. I know I came in through the balcony, but you made me do it by not opening the door.
CHEMIST'S WIFE	You can't stay here. I'll pay for you to go somewhere else!

DOÑA TERITA empties her purse into her lap. A needle case, some keys, and a ball of wool spill out with a few coins, which she begins to count.

JOHNNY BLUSTER	You haven't got much change, Doña Terita.
CHEMIST'S WIFE	Two *pesetas* is more than enough!
JOHNNY BLUSTER	It's going to take more than that! I'll have you know I only ever stay in the very best hotels. We can discuss it further, if you insist. You should

	con un servidor para no olvidarlo en la vida. Si usted me otorgase alguna de sus dulces miradas, tendría el comprobante.
LA BOTICARIA	¡Respete usted la memoria de mi esposo! ¡No más escarnios!
JUANITO VENTOLERA	Es usted una viuda por demás acalorada.
LA BOTICARIA	¡Váyase usted!
JUANITO VENTOLERA	Estoy aquí para recoger el bombín y el bastón del difunto. ¡Me los ha legado! ¿Reconoce usted el terno? ¡Me lo ha legado! ¡Un barbián el patrón! ¡Se antojó disfrazarse con mi rayadillo, para darle una broma a San Pedro! Repare usted el terno que yo visto. Hemos changado y vengo por el bombín y el bastón de borlas. Va usted a dármelos. Se los pido en nombre del llorado cadáver. Levante usted la cabeza. Descúbrase los ojos. Irrádieme usted una mirada.

Hace en torno de LA BOTICARIA *un bordo de gallo pinturero con castañuelas y compases de baile.* LA BOTICARIA *aspa los brazos en el ruedo de las faldas, grita perlática.*

LA BOTICARIA	¡Cristo bendito! ¡Noche de espantos! ¡Esto es un mal sueño! ¡Sueño renegado! ¡Niño! ¡Niño! ¿Dónde estás? ¡Mójame las sienes! ¡Échame agua en la cara! ¡El espasmódico! ¡No te vayas!
JUANITO VENTOLERA	¡Doña Terita, deje usted esos formulismos de novela! ¡Propios delirios gástricos! El finado difunto me ha solicitado el rayadillo, para no llevarse prenda de estima al Infierno. Los gritos de usted están por demás. ¡Delirios gástricos! ¡Bastón y bombín para irme de naja, que me espera una gachí de mistó! Usted tampoco está mala. ¡Bastón y bombín! ¡Doña Terita, va usted a recrearse mirándome!

know that your dearly departed took pains to ensure that his humble servant would not be forgotten in this life. If you would only grant me a look from those sweet eyes, you would understand.

CHEMIST'S WIFE   Show some respect for my husband's memory! Stop making fun of me!

JOHNNY BLUSTER   You're very excitable for a widow.

CHEMIST'S WIFE   Go away!

JOHNNY BLUSTER   I'm here to collect the deceased's hat and cane. He left them to me! Do you recognise the suit? He left it to me! What a mighty good chap he was! He took it into his head to dress up in my striped uniform, just to give old Saint Peter a laugh! Look at the suit I'm wearing. We swapped and so I'm here for the hat and the cane with the tassels. You're going to give them to me. I'm asking for them in the name of your dearly departed. Lift your head. Look at me. Burn me up with your eyes.

He struts and swaggers like a cockerel around the CHEMIST'S WIFE, pretending to dance and play the castanets. Marooned inside the ring of her skirts, DOÑA TERITA gesticulates wildly and screams hysterically.

CHEMIST'S WIFE   Christ almighty, what a night! Horror after horror! It's a nightmare, a hideous dream! Where's the boy? Where are you? Bring me a cold compress! Splash some water on my face! Bring me my tablets! Don't leave me!

JOHNNY BLUSTER   Doña Terita, you're not the heroine of some cheap novel. You must have gastric fever. The recently deceased asked for my striped uniform, so that he wouldn't have to take his best suit to hell. Your screams are over the top. It's gastric fever, believe me! The hat and the cane if you want me to scram, so I don't keep my sweet chippy waiting! As a matter of fact you're not too hard on the eye yourself. Hat and cane! Doña Terita,

LA BOTICARIA	¡Niño, dame el rosario! ¡Llévame a la cama! ¡Échale un aspergio de agua bendita! ¡Anda suelto el Maligno! ¡Me baila alrededor con negro revuelo! ¡Esposo mío, si estás enojado, desenójate! ¡Tendrás los mejores sufragios! ¡Aunque monten a la luna! ¡Niño, llévame a la cama!
JUANITO VENTOLERA	¡Niño, vamos a ello y cachea un pañuelo para ponerle mordaza! ¡Vivo y sin atolondrarse! ¡Ya te llegará la tuya!

DOÑA TERITA se desmaya, asomando un zancajo. El virote mandilón hipa turulato. juanillo ventolera le sacude por la nariz.

EL GALOPÍN	¡Ay! ¡Ay! ¡Ay!
JUANITO VENTOLERA	¡Una soga!
EL GALOPÍN	¿Y de dónde la saco?
JUANITO VENTOLERA	De la pelleja.

Le arranca el mandilón y lo hace tiras. el GALOPÍN queda en almilla: Un mamarracho, con gran culera remendada, tirantes y alpargates. Se limpia los ojos.

EL GALOPÍN	¡Para eso un vendaje Barré!
JUANITO VENTOLERA	Ese pío llega retrasado. Vamos con la patrona a tumbarla en el catre.

EL GALOPÍN se mueve, obediente a la voluntad del soldado. Sacan a la desmayada del ruedo haldudo, y la llevan en volandas. Por la cinturilla del jubón negro, la camisa ondula su faldeta. Se apaga la luz oportunamente.

	you'll crack up when you see me!
CHEMIST'S WIFE	Give me my rosary, boy! Help me into bed! Sprinkle it with holy water! Satan is among us! He is dancing around me beating his black wings! Oh husband, if you are angry, let me appease you! I'll give you the best send-off imaginable, even if it costs me the moon! Help me into bed, boy!
JOHNNY BLUSTER	Come on, let's get on with it, and find me a handkerchief to gag her with. Wake up, don't just stand there! It'll be your turn soon!

DOÑA TERITA faints, her heel sticking out below her skirts. The hopeless CALLOW YOUTH hiccups with fear. JOHNNY BLUSTER shakes him by the nose.

CALLOW YOUTH	Ow! Ow! Ow!
JOHNNY BLUSTER	I need a gag!
CALLOW YOUTH	And where am I supposed to get one?
JOHNNY BLUSTER	From your own hide, you animal.

He rips off the CALLOW YOUTH's jacket and shreds it, leaving him in his waistcoat, braces and espadrilles, with a darned patch on the seat of his trousers. He looks a buffoon. He snivels and wipes his eyes.

| CALLOW YOUTH | You should use a proper bandage for that! |
| JOHNNY BLUSTER | You just haven't caught on to the latest techniques. Come on, time for sleeping beauty here to say night-night. |

The CALLOW YOUTH responds obediently to the soldier's instructions. They lift the unconscious DOÑA TERITA out of the hoop of her skirts and support her between them. Her blouse flaps beneath the waistband of her black bodice. The light goes out opportunely.

ESCENA SÉPTIMA

La borrosa silueta por el entresijo de callejones, entrevista la casa del pecado. Bastón y bombín, botas con grillos en las suelas. Esguinces de avinado. En la sala baja las manflotas – flores en el peinado, batas con lazos y volantes – cecean tras de las rejas a cuantos pasan. JUANITO VENTOLERA, con un esguince en la puerta.

JUANITO VENTOLERA	¡Vengo a dejaros la plata! ¡Se me ha puesto convidaros a todas! Si no hay piano, se busca. ¡Aquí se responde con cartera! ¡Madre Priora, quiero llevarme una gachí! ¡Redimirla! ¿Dónde está esa garza enjaulada?
LA DAIFA	¡Buena la traes! ¡Te desconocía sin las cruces del pecho! ¿O tú no eres el punto que me habló la noche pasada?
JUANITO VENTOLERA	¡Juanillo Ventolera, repatriado de Cubita Libre!
LA DAIFA	¿Por qué no traes puestas las cruces?
JUANITO VENTOLERA	Se las traspasé a un fiambre. ¡Con ellas podrá darse pisto entre las Benditas del Purgatorio!
LA DAIFA	¡No hagas escarnio! ¡Entre las benditas hago cuenta que tengo a mi madre!
JUANITO VENTOLERA	¿Y tu papá, de dónde te escribe?
LA DAIFA	A ése no lo quiere ni el Diablo.
JUANITO VENTOLERA	¡Sujeto de mérito!
LA DAIFA	¡Mira qué ilusión! ¡Cuando te vi llegar, se me ha representado! ¡Bombín y bastón! ¡Majo que te vienes!
JUANITO VENTOLERA	¡Una hembra tan barbi no pide menos!
LA DAIFA	¡Algo más gordo era el finado!
JUANITO VENTOLERA	Aciertas más de lo que sospechas, lo ha llevado antes un muerto. Se lo he pedido para venir a camelarte.

SCENE SEVEN

A blurred figure weaves its way through the labyrinth of alleyways that secretes the house of sin. It carries a hat and a cane, and two crickets in the soles of its boots. It rolls drunkenly. The hookers, wearing frilly gowns and flowers in their hair, whisper lewdly to the passers-by through the iron bars of the window. JOHNNY BLUSTER stumbles and lurches in the doorway.

JOHNNY BLUSTER	I've come to give you the money I promised! Drinks are on me! Where's the piano? We need a piano! A full wallet is the way to your hearts, and yours truly's got one! Mother Superior, I've come for the girl! I'm here to redeem her! Where is my caged turtledove?[15]
COURTESAN	You're looking good! I didn't recognise you without all your medals! You are the chap that was here the other night, aren't you?
JOHNNY BLUSTER	I am Johnny Bluster, back from a *Cuba Libre*!
COURTESAN	Why aren't you wearing your medals?
JOHNNY BLUSTER	I gave them to a corpse. He can show them off to the holy souls in Purgatory!
COURTESAN	That's not funny! One of those souls is my mother's.
JOHNNY BLUSTER	What about your father, where does he stamp his postcards?
COURTESAN	Not even the devil wants him.
JOHNNY BLUSTER	I like him already!
COURTESAN	It's amazing; when I saw you I thought it was him! It's the hat and the cane. You're looking dapper!
JOHNNY BLUSTER	A good-looking girl like you deserves nothing less.
COURTESAN	Whoever the dead man was, he was a bit fatter than you.
JOHNNY BLUSTER	Truer than you might think. A dead man did wear this suit before me. I asked him to let me have it so I could come and woo you.

LA DAIFA	Deja la guasa. ¡Vaya un terno! ¡Y los forros de primera!
JUANITO VENTOLERA	¡Una ganga!
LA DAIFA	¡Pues si voy a decirte verdad, mejor me caías con el rayadillo y las cruces en el pecho!
JUANITO VENTOLERA	¡Las mujeres os deslumbráis con apariencias panolis! ¡Todas al modo de mariposas! Las cruces, de paisano, no visten.
LA DAIFA	¡Me gustabas más con las cruces!
JUANITO VENTOLERA	¡No visten! ¡Vamos, niña, a ponerme los ojos tiernos!... ¡A mudar de tocata, y a darme el opio con tus miradas!
LA DAIFA	¿Y si me negase? ¿Me declaré por un acaso tu fiel esclava? ¡A mí no me chulea ni el rey de los odios, para cuantimás Juanillo Ventolera!
JUANITO VENTOLERA	Por achares no entro, paloma. Soy piloto de todos los mares y no me cogen de sobresalto cambios de veleta. Déjame paso, que me está haciendo tilín aquella morocha.
LA DAIFA	Primero convida, y si te duele hacer la jarra, yo pago los cafeses.
JUANITO VENTOLERA	¿Con copa?
LA DAIFA	Copa y cajetilla de habanos.
JUANITO VENTOLERA	Dirás luego que te chuleo, cuando eres tú propia quien me busca las vueltas, como a Cristo la María Magdalena. ¡Yo pago los cafeses y cuanto se tercie! ¡Y si te hallo de mi gusto te redimo! ¡Se responde con cartera! ¡Madre Celeste, a cerrar las puertas! ¡Esta noche reina aquí Juanito Ventolera!

El bulto encapuchado del farol y el chuzo aparece por la esquina, LA MADRE CELESTE arruga el ruedo de las faldas, metiéndose por medio entre LA DAIFA y el soldado.

COURTESAN	You're having me on. What a suit! The lining's top quality!
JOHNNY BLUSTER	It was a bargain!
COURTESAN	Though to tell you the truth, I liked you better with your uniform and your medals.
JOHNNY BLUSTER	You women, you're impressed by such stupid things! You're like butterflies! Medals on a civilian suit...!
COURTESAN	I liked you better with them on!
JOHNNY BLUSTER	But this suit is simply spiffing! Now come on, dollface, give me those come-to-bed eyes! Change the tune will you, and show me what you're made of!
COURTESAN	And what if I don't want to? I don't remember declaring my everlasting devotion to you. Nobody leeches off me, least of all little Johnny Bluster!
JOHNNY BLUSTER	Don't think you can make me beg, sweetheart. I've sailed rougher seas than these and I'm used to the wind changing. So move over, I think I fancy that dark-haired lovely over there.
COURTESAN	First invite me for a coffee, and if your arms aren't long enough for your pockets I'll do the honours.
JOHNNY BLUSTER	And you'll buy the drinks?
COURTESAN	And a pack of Cubans.
JOHNNY BLUSTER	Then you'll say I'm leeching off you, when you're the one taking advantage of my good nature, like Mary Magdalene and Christ. I'll pay for the coffees and anything else you fancy! And if you play your cards right I might just redeem you! A fat wallet is all I need! Celestial Mother, shut the doors! Tonight Johnny Bluster is king of the whores!

The hooded shape of a lamp and a nightwatchman's pointed stick appear round the corner. The CELESTIAL MOTHER gathers up her round skirts and places herself between the COURTESAN and the soldier.

LA MADRE	¡A no mover escándalo! ¡Niña, al adentro! ¡Basta de changüí, que palique en puerta sólo gana resfriados! Si este boquillero quiere juerga, que afloje los busiles.
JUANITO VENTOLERA	Tengo en la bolsa un kilo de billetaje.
LA MADRE	Con que saques un veragua...
JUANITO VENTOLERA	¡Voy a cegarte!

Se desabotona y palpa el pecho. Del bolsillo interior extrae una carta cerrada. Se mete por la sala de daifas con el sobre en la mano, buscando luz para leerlo: Queda en el círculo de la lámpara.

JUANITO VENTOLERA	Correo de difuntos. Sin franqueo. Señor Don Sócrates Galindo.
LA DAIFA	Deja las burlas. ¿De dónde conoces a ese sujeto?
JUANITO VENTOLERA	¡Mi ex patrón!
LA DAIFA	¿El boticario de Calle Nueva?
JUANITO VENTOLERA	El mismo.
LA DAIFA	¡Qué enredo malvado! ¿Te habló de mí? ¿Cómo averiguaste el lazo que conmigo tiene?
JUANITO VENTOLERA	No entro por achares. De tu pasado, morena, no se me da nada.
LA DAIFA	Pues tú me has tirado la pulla.
JUANITO VENTOLERA	He leído el nombre que viene en el sobre.
LA DAIFA	¿Y esa carta, cómo está en tus manos? ¿Quieres aclarármelo?
JUANITO VENTOLERA	Venía en el terno.

Las niñas se acunan en las mecedoras: Fuman cigarrillos de soldado, deleitándose con pereza galocha; un hilo de humo en la raja pintada de la boca. La tía coruja, que se recose el zancajo bajo la escalerilla, susurra con guiño, quebrando la hebra.

LA BRUJA	¿Cuántos cafeses?
JUANITO VENTOLERA	Para toda la concurrencia.

MADAM	You'll get tongues wagging if you stay out here! Come on you, inside! That's quite enough nonsense. You'll catch your deaths standing around chatting in doorways. If this jinal wants some fun, he'll have to cough up.
JOHNNY BLUSTER	Reverend Mother, I can hardly stand for the weight of my wallet.
MADAM	Better show us a fat wad, then.
JOHNNY BLUSTER	Just you wait…!

He unbuttons his jackets and feels around inside. He pulls a sealed letter from the inside pocket. He walks into the whores' parlour with the envelope in his hand, looking for some light to read it by: he finds the circular glow of a lamp.

JOHNNY BLUSTER	Postal service for the dead. No stamp. Addressed to one Don Socrates Galindo.
COURTESAN	Stop it. How do you know that man?
JOHNNY BLUSTER	He was my landlord!
COURTESAN	The chemist?
JOHNNY BLUSTER	The very same.
COURTESAN	This is ugly! Did he tell you about me? How did you find out?
JOHNNY BLUSTER	Don't try and make me jealous again, darling. You can keep your sordid past to yourself.
COURTESAN	You brought it up! Just to humiliate me, I suppose!
JOHNNY BLUSTER	I only read out the name on the envelope.
COURTESAN	How did you get hold of that letter? Tell me!
JOHNNY BLUSTER	It was in the pocket of this suit.

The girls ease back and forth in their rocking chairs, smoking soldiers' cigarettes with indolent pleasure. Thin trails of smoke escape from the painted gashes of their mouths. The owl-witch mutters and grimaces as she darns her stockings in the stairway, snapping the thread with her teeth.

WITCH	How many coffees?
JOHNNY BLUSTER	One for every member of the audience.

LA MADRE	¡Alumbra por delante el pago, moreno!
JUANITO VENTOLERA	Madre Celeste, tengo para comprarte todo el ganado.

JUANITO VENTOLERA posa la carta en el velador, entre la baraja y el plato de habichuelas: Torna a palparse los bolsillos, y muestra un fajo de billetes. Se guarda los billetes, rasga el sobre de la carta y saca un pliego de escritura torcida.

JUANITO VENTOLERA	«Querido padre: Por la presente considere el arrepentimiento de esta su hija, que se reputa como la más desgraciada de las mujeres».
LA DAIFA	¡Esa carta yo la escribí! ¡Mi carta! Juanillo Ventolera, rompe ese papel. ¡No leas más! ¡Si te pagan por venir a clavarme ese puñal, ya tienes cumplido! ¡Dame esa carta!
JUANITO VENTOLERA	¿Tú la escribiste?
LA DAIFA	Yo misma.
JUANITO VENTOLERA	¡Miau! ¡Vas a darte por hija del difunto!
LA DAIFA	¡Difunto mi padre!
JUANITO VENTOLERA	¡Qué enredo macanudo!
LA DAIFA	¡Responde! ¿Difunto mi padre?
JUANITO VENTOLERA	¿El boticario de Calle Nueva?
LA DAIFA	¡Justamente!
JUANITO VENTOLERA	¡Mi ex patrón! Hoy ha recibido tierra el autor de tus días. Ayer estiró el remo. ¡Niña, los dos heredamos!
LA DAIFA	¡Qué relajo de guasa!
JUANITO VENTOLERA	¡Este flux tan majo le ha servido de mortaja! Me propuso la changa para darle una broma a San Pedro. ¡Has heredado! ¡Eres huérfana! ¡Luz de donde el sol la toma, no te mires más para desmayarte!
LA DAIFA	¡Ay, mi padre!
LA MADRE	¡Sujetadle las manos para que no se arañe el físico! ¡Que huela vinagre! ¡Satanás de los Infiernos, éstos son los cafeses a que convidabas!

| MADAM | Let's see what you've got first, my lovely! |
| JOHNNY BLUSTER | Celestial Mother, I could buy every cow in the herd. |

JOHNNY BLUSTER places the letter on the side table, between a pack of cards and a plate of beans. He feels around in his pockets again and pulls out a wad of banknotes. He puts the cash away, opens the envelope and takes out a letter written in a crooked hand.

JOHNNY BLUSTER	"Dear Father, I beg you to acknowledge that I, your daughter, sincerely and wholeheartedly repent of my actions, and consider myself the most unfortunate of women."
COURTESAN	I wrote that letter! That's my letter! Johnny Bluster, I beg you, tear it up! Don't read any more of it! If you've been paid to come and plant a knife in my heart, consider it done! Give me the letter!
JOHNNY BLUSTER	You wrote it?
COURTESAN	Yes!
JOHNNY BLUSTER	Well, well! Don't tell me you're the dead man's daughter!
COURTESAN	My father's dead?
JOHNNY BLUSTER	What a superb coincidence!
COURTESAN	Answer me! Is my father dead?
JOHNNY BLUSTER	The chemist?
COURTESAN	Yes!
JOHNNY BLUSTER	My former landlord! The man who spawned you has today gone six feet under. He kicked the bucket yesterday. And we stand to inherit!
COURTESAN	If this is a joke it's cruel and indecent!
JOHNNY BLUSTER	And this is the tinkerty-tonk suit he was buried in! He suggested a swap so that he could give Saint Peter a laugh. You are an orphan! You can claim your legacy! Oh light that lights the sun, feel free to faint with happiness![16]
COURTESAN	Oh, oh, my father!
MADAM	Grab her hands so she doesn't scratch her face! Bring the smelling salts! Satan in Hell, so much for buying us all a coffee!

La tía coruja acude con un botellín. Dos NIÑAS sujetan las manos de la desmayada: Enseña las ligas, se le suelta el moño, suspira con espasmo histérico. JUANITO VENTOLERA, en tanto la asisten, hace lectura de la carta.

JUANITO VENTOLERA

«Querido padre:

Por la presente considere usted el arrepentimiento de esta hija que se reputa como la más desgraciada de las mujeres. Una mujer abandonada, considere, padre mío, que es puesta en los brazos del pecado. Considere, padre mío, qué cosa tan triste buscar trabajo y hallar cerradas todas las puertas. Así que usted verá. Considere, padre mío, que, falta de recursos, muerta de hambre sin este trato de mi cuerpo aborrecido, estuve en el hospital sacramentada, y todos allí me daban por muerta. ¡Vea, padre mío, cómo me veo castigada! Recibí el recado que me mandó por la asistenta, y debo decirle no ser verdad que yo arrastre su honra, pues con esa mira cambié mi nombre, y digo en todas partes que me llamo Ernestina. No tiene, pues, nada que recelar, que siempre fui hija amantísima, y no iba ahora a dejar de serlo. En cuanto a lo otro que me manda decir, también lo haré. Conforme estoy en irme adonde no se sepa de mi vida. Pero tengo una deuda en la casa donde estoy, y el ama me retiene la ropa. Sin eso, ya me hubiese ido a Lisboa. Dicen que allí las españolas son muy estimadas. Las compañeras que conocen aquello lo ponen por cima de Barcelona. El viaje cuesta diez duros. Tocante a la deuda, con pagar la mitad ya me dejan sacar el baúl. Padre mío, levánteme su maldición, mire por esta hija. No volveré a molestarle. La cantidad que le señalo es la menos con que puedo arreglarme, y a su buen corazón se encomienda esta su hija que lo es,

Ernestina. Así es como deben preguntar.

Casa de la Carmelitana, Entremuros, 37».

UNA NIÑA ¡Está bien puesta la carta!

OTRA NIÑA ¡La sacó del Manual!

LA MADRE Juanillo, hojea el billetaje. Después de este folletín los cafeses son obligados.

The owl-witch runs over with a little bottle. Two girls hold down the swooning COURTESAN's hands. Her skirt rides up over her suspenders; her hair has come loose; she gasps and sobs hysterically. JOHNNY BLUSTER reads the letter aloud while the women assist her.

JOHNNY BLUSTER

"Dear Father,

I beg you to acknowledge that I, your daughter, sincerely and wholeheartedly repent of my actions, and consider myself the most unfortunate of women. Please consider, father, that I am an abandoned woman, forced into the ways of sin. Consider, father, what a terrible thing it is for a young woman to seek employment and to have every door slammed in her face. What choice did I have? Consider, father, that without any means to support myself, half starved because I wouldn't consent to sell my poor body, I found myself in hospital, where they gave me the last rites and expected me to die. See, father, how I have been punished! I read the message you sent me, and it isn't true that I have dishonoured you and dragged your name through the mud, because I was careful to change my name, and everyone here knows me as Ernestina. So you have nothing to fear, because I have always been and will ever be your devoted daughter. As for the other thing you asked of me, I will do it. I am going away so you will never have to hear of me again. But I owe some money to the mistress of the house, and she is keeping my clothes as a surety. Otherwise I would already have gone to Lisbon. I am told that Spanish girls are held in high esteem there. The girls who know these things say it's even better than Barcelona. The journey will cost ten *duros*. As for the money I owe, if I can just pay off half they'll give me back my clothes. Dear father, please forgive me and look kindly on your own daughter. I won't trouble you again. I ask only for this small sum, the smallest I need to get away from here, and so I commit myself to your kind heart.

Your loving daughter, Ernestina."

A GIRL	It's not a bad letter!
ANOTHER GIRL	Not bad? It's textbook!
MADAM	Johnny, get your stash out. After this little melodrama we'll all be needing a cup of coffee.

NOTES

1   Valle-Inclán refers to her as a 'daifa', meaning 'concubine'. I have used the word 'courtesan' to echo the ironic implication that she is among members of high society (which, of course, she is not).

2   Johnny Bluster is a soldier returning to Spain after the Cuban War of Independence (1895–98) and the ensuing Spanish-American war (1898). Spain suffered a humiliating defeat in this war that defined a generation, and the loss of its last overseas colonies.

3   The surnames of these characters (Maside, Ricote and Maluenda) are also the names of Spanish municipalities in the regions of Galicia, Murcia and Aragón.

4   Valle-Inclán describes the Witch here as a 'coima': according to Ricardo Senabre, this word refers to the person in charge of the brothel and is taken from the 'lenguaje de germanía' or underworld slang of the Spanish Golden Age. (1990, 44)

5   'Es muy contraria muy suerte': Although ostensibly the courtesan is saying here, 'I've been so unfortunate', there may also be a pun on the bullfighting term 'la suerte contraria', which refers to the position the bullfighter takes up during the final part of the fight when he is preparing to kill the bull. This might indicate a degree of disingenuousness on the part of the Courtesan as she writes the letter to her father (also suggested by her assertion that it would 'make a rock weep'). For that reason I have tried to indicate that the she is not merely bemoaning her bad luck but also making an attempt to turn improve her situation by appealing to her father.

6   The term 'mambí' is applied in Cuba to those who fought for independence against the Spanish forces in 1895–98.

7   'La bandera es la oreja': literally, 'the flag is the ear'. Manuel Aznar Soler explains that this is a bullfighting term referring to the ear of the bull, given away as a prize at the end of the fight. (1992b, 77).

8   The word Johnny uses is 'camama', meaning 'trick' or 'joke', by which he seems to mean that draping coffins in the flag is a meaningless show in any case.

9   François Claudius Koenigstein, known as Ravachol (1859–1892), was a French anarchist. He was executed in 1892 for a series of attacks on right-wing judges. His first criminal act was the robbing of a grave (Senabre 1990, 51).

10   Senabre is unsure of the significance of the 'duro romanonista,' which is named after the liberal politician the Conde de Romanones. He suggests that it means a coin from the capital, given that Romanones, who was notorious for his meanness, was mayor of Madrid for a time (1990, 51).

11   Alfonso XIII was King of Spain from 1886 until he was deposed by the Second Republic in 1931. His mother María Cristina was regent during his minority. Valle-Inclán is of course implying here that the King is a liar.

12   According to Senabre, the 'ojo del boticario' was a display case containing expensive and potentially toxic medicines, frequently painted with an eye (1990, 57).

13   They are alluding here to Don Juan's famous invitation of the Stone Guest to dinner.

14   *Blanco y Negro* was an illustrated magazine founded in 1891 by Torcuato Luca de

Tena and Álvarez Ossorio, devoted to publishing new narrative fiction alongside features on art, culture, bullfighting, sport and national and international news. The enormous popular success of this magazine led to the creation of the royalist daily ABC. *Blanco y Negro* survived as an independent weekly until 1939, with the exception of the years 1931–36, when it was banned by the Republican government. It was re-launched in 1957 and survived until 1988, when it became the Sunday supplement of the ABC. In 2002 it became the ABC's cultural supplement and in 2005 it was renamed *ABCD Las Artes y las Letras*. As a royalist and eminently bourgeois publication at the time that Valle-Inclán was writing, the playwright is clearly satirising its content through the rapturous account of the absurd barber.

15 '¿Dónde está esa garza enjaulada?' Valle-Inclán is here quoting a famous line from Zorrilla's *Don Juan Tenorio*: 'Pobre garza enjaulada,/ dentro la jaula nacida' [Poor caged heron, / born in its cage] (Act II, sc. ix). Though a 'garza' is a heron, I've rendered it as 'turtledove' for the romantic and slightly twee associations that word has in English.

16 '¡Luz de donde el sol la toma…!' ['Light that lights the sun…'] Valle-Inclán is again quoting Zorrilla's *Don Juan Tenorio*, Act III, sc. iii).

LA HIJA DEL CAPITÁN

THE CAPTAIN'S DAUGHTER

Dramatis Personae

El golfante del organillo y una mucama negra mandinga

La poco-gusto, el cosmético y EL TAPABOCAS, pícaros de las afueras

Un HORCHATERO

La Sinibalda, que atiende por LA SINI, y su padre, el CAPITÁN CHULETAS de SARGENTO

Un GENERAL glorioso y los cuatro compadres: EL POLLO DE CARTAGENA, el banquero TRAPISONDAS, el ex MINISTRO marchoso y el TONGUISTA donostiarra

El ASISTENTE dEL CAPITÁN

Un CAMARERO de café

El sastre penela y EL BATUCO, acróbatas del código

Un CAMASTRÓN, un QUITOLIS, un CHULAPO acreditado en el tapete verde, un POLLO BABIECA y un REPÓRTER, socios de Bellas Artes

TOTÓ, oficial de Húsares, Ayudante dEL GENERAL, y otro AYUDANTE

El BRIGADIER Frontaura y EL CORONEL CAMARASA

DOÑA SIMPLICIA, dama intelectual

Su ILUSTRÍSIMA, Obispo *in partibus*

Una BEATA, un PATRIOTA, un PROFESOR DE HISTORIA

El MONARCA

Un LORITO de ultramar

Organillos y charangas

Dramatis Personae

An organ-grinding BUM and a mandinka MAID[1]

TASTELESS, PRETTY-BOY and MENACE, three young troublemakers from
    outside town

A DRINKS VENDOR selling *horchata*[2]

Sinibalda, known as SINI, as her father CAPTAIN CUTLETS the butcher

A glorious GENERAL and four cronies: the SPRING CHICKEN; MR RUMPUS
    the Catalan banker; a spritely EX-MINISTER; and a BASQUE CON MAN

The CAPTAIN's AIDE-DE-CAMP

A café WAITER

The TAILOR and DANDY, legal contortionists

The DODGER, the DIVER, the LOUT OF THE GREEN BAIZE, a BOZO and a
    REPORTER, members of the Circle of Fine Arts

TOTO, officer of the Hussars and Adjutant to the General

A second ADJUTANT to the General

A BRIGADIER and a COLONEL

MRS SIMPLETON, a lady of intellect

His Excellency the BISHOP *in partibus*

A DEVOUT LADY, a PATRIOTIC GENTLEMAN, and a TEACHER OF HISTORY

The MONARCH

An imported PARROT

Barrel organs and sounding brass

ESCENA PRIMERA

Madrid Moderno: En un mirador espioja el alón verdigualda un loro ultramarino: La siesta: Calle jaulera de minúsculos hoteles. Persianas verdes. Enredaderas. Resol en la calle. En yermos solares la barraca de horchata y melones, con el obeso levantino en mangas de camisa. – Un organillo.– Al golfante del manubrio, calzones de odalisca y andares presumidos de botas nuevas, le asoma un bucle fuera de la gorrilla, con estudiado estrágalo, y sobre el hombro le hace morisquetas el pico verderol del pañolito gargantero. – Por la verja de un jardín se concierta con una negra mucama.

EL LORO	¡Cubanita canela!
EL GOLFANTE	Ese amigo me ha dado el primer quién vive. Oírlo y caer en la cuenta de que andaba por aquí el Capitán. Después he visto asomar el moño de la Sini. No sé si me habrá reconocido.
LA MUCAMA	Es mucho el cambio. Si usted no se me descubre, yo no le saco. La niña, sin duda, tendrá más presente su imagen.
EL GOLFANTE	¡Cómo me la ha pegado! Ésa ha sido cegada por los papiros del tío ladrón.
LA MUCAMA	Más es el ruido.
EL GOLFANTE	Ya sé que no pagáis una cuenta y que tu amo tira el pego en su casa. Otro Huerto del Francés estáis armando. ¡Buena fama os dan en el barrio!
LA MUCAMA	¡Qué chance! Estamos en un purito centro de comadreo.
EL LORO	¡Cubanita canela!
EL GOLFANTE	Ese charlatán es un bando municipal sobre la ventana de la Sini. La andaba buscando loco por esas calles, y aquí estaba esperándome el lorito con su letrero. ¡Impensadamente volvía a ponerse en mi camino la condenada sombra de la Sini! ¡Aquí está mi perdición! Entra y dile que el punto organillero desea obsequiarla con un tango. Que

SCENE ONE

A bay window in Modern Madrid,[3] where an imported PARROT plucks fleas from its green and gold wing. A cagey street of dolls houses at siesta time: green blinds; climbing plants; the afternoon sun pounding the hot street. The DRINKS VENDOR, an obese Levantine selling melons and horchata, tends his stall in a dilapidated yard. He is in his shirtsleeves. A barrel organ. Wearing the trousers of an odalisque, the organ-grinding BUM struts vainly in his new boots. From under his cap, a lock of hair curls artfully on his forehead; a neckerchief pecks playfully at his shoulder like a yellowhammer's beak. He and the MAID are setting the world to rights over the garden fence.

PARROT	Latin lovely! Latin lovely!
BUM	Our little parrot friend gave the game away, screeching away like some crazy drill sergeant. I knew I'd find the Captain around here somewhere. I caught sight of the back of Sini's head too. I don't know if she recognised me.
MAID	You look different! I wouldn't have known you. But then I'd forgot all about you.
BUM	She really took me for a mug! And now she's gone off with that thieving bastard just because he waved some cash under her nose!
MAID	Come now, I hear there is more to it than that.
BUM	And I hear your boss has got a scam going and never pays what he owes. And that he robs all his clients and then chucks them in the river. You're really making a name for yourselves!
MAID	Cha! This town is full of tittle-tattle!
PARROT	Latin lovely!
BUM	That parrot's like a banner at Sini's window. I nearly lost my mind searching the streets for her, and all along it was waiting for me here, like a sign. I thought I'd never see her again. Damn her to hell! She'll be the end of me! Go in and tell her the nice man with the organ wants to ask her to dance. Tell her if she's a good girl she'll come

	salga, como es de política, a darme las gracias y proponer el más de su gusto. Y si no sale será que prefiere oír todo el repertorio. Recomiéndale que no sea tan filarmónica.
LA MUCAMA	¡Apártese! Tenemos bucaneros en la costa.

Disimulábase la negra mandinga regando las macetas, y el pirante del organillo batió la Marcha de Cádiz. Salía, en traje de paisano, EL CAPITÁN Sinibaldo Pérez: Flux de alpaca negra, camisa de azulinos almidones, las botas militares un abierto compás de charolados brillos, el bombín sobre la ceja, el manatí jugando en los dedos. Dos puntos holgazanes y una golfa andariega que refrescan en la barraca del levantino, hacen su comentario a espaldas del CAPITÁN. LA POCO-GUSTO, le dicen a la mozuela, y a los dos pirantes, Pepe el cosmético y Toño EL TAPABOCAS.

LA POCO-GUSTO	¡Qué postinero!
EL COSMÉTICO	Por algo es Chuletas de Sargento.
EL HORCHATERO	Esa machada se la cuelgan.
EL COSMÉTICO	¿Que no es verdad, y está sumariado?
EL HORCHATERO	Las Ordenanzas Militares son muy severas, y los ranchos con criadillas de prisioneros están más penados que entre moros comer tocino. Tocante al Capitán, yo no le creo hombre para darse esa manutención.
EL TAPABOCAS	¡Que no fuese guateque diario, estamos en ello! Pero él propio se alaba.
EL HORCHATERO	¡Boquerón que es el compadre!
LA POCO-GUSTO	¿Y el proceso?
EL HORCHATERO	¡Che! Por tirar la descargada.
EL COSMÉTICO	A mí no me presenta un mérito tan alto, estando de buen paladar, comer chuletas. ¿Que son de sargento? Como si fueran de cordero. ¡En estando de gusto!
EL TAPABOCAS	¿Y por qué razón no van a saber buenas las chuletas de sargento mambís?
LA POCO-GUSTO	¡Se podrán comer, pero buenas!...
EL TAPABOCAS	Buenas. ¿Por qué no?

| | out and thank me and we can dance the tango or whatever she fancies. And if she doesn't come out I'll assume she wants me to play my whole repertoire. You might want to advise her not be so philharmonic. |
| MAID | Look out! Pirates ahoy! |

The MAID *starts busily watering the plants. The organ grinder strikes up the Marcha de Cádiz, a jaunty favourite of the light opera.[4] The* CAPTAIN *emerges in his civvies: a soft black woollen suit, a bluish starched shirt, his military boots a pair of shiny open compasses, his bowler hat cocked over one eye. He is fingering his riding crop. Two indolent youths and a streetwalker are taking refreshment at the Levantine's stall; they talk behind the* CAPTAIN's *back. The young woman is known as* TASTELESS; *the two youths are* PRETTY-BOY *and* MENACE.

TASTELESS	He fancies himself a bit!
PRETTY-BOY	They don't call him Cutlets the Butcher for nothing.
DRINKS VENDOR	It's all swagger. He didn't really do it.
PRETTY-BOY	You reckon? They're going to try him for it!
DRINKS VENDOR	The army has very strict rules. And serving up prisoners' goolies at the snake pit is a no-no![5] It's worse than for a moor to eat bacon. Anyway, I don't think the Captain is man enough to eat a soldier's crown jewels.
MENACE	Maybe not every day! But he boasts about it!
DRINKS VENDOR	He's full of it.
TASTELESS	What about the trial then?
DRINKS VENDOR	Like throwing away at cards.
PRETTY-BOY	I don't see what all the fuss is about. So he filleted a sergeant! It's no different to lamb. So long as it tastes good…!
MENACE	And why shouldn't a *mambi*[6] cutlet taste good?
TASTELESS	I'm sure it's delicious!
MENACE	Of course it's delicious!

EL HORCHATERO	Con mucho vino, con mucha guindilla, por una apuesta, limpias de grasas, lo magro magro, casi convengo.
EL COSMÉTICO	Y así habrá sido.
EL HORCHATERO	Ni eso!
EL TAPABOCAS	Pues se lo han acumulado como un guateque diario y tiene una sumaria a pique de salir expulsado de la Milicia.
EL HORCHATERO	¡Bien seguro se halla! Para que el proceso duerma, la hija se acuesta con el Gobernador Militar.
LA POCO-GUSTO	La dormida de la hija por la dormida del expediente.
EL COSMÉTICO	¡Una baza de órdago a la grande!
EL HORCHATERO	No llegan las pagas, hay mucho vicio y se cultiva la finca de las mujeres.
EL COSMÉTICO	Quien tiene la suerte de esas fincas. Menda es huérfano.
EL HORCHATERO	Te casas y pones la parienta al toreo.
EL COSMÉTICO	¿Y si no vale para la lidia?
LA POCO-GUSTO	Búscala capeada. ¡Mira la Sini, al timoteo con el andoba del organillo!

LA SINIBALDA, peinador con lazos, falda bajera, moñas en los zapatos, un clavel en el pelo, conversaba por la verja del jardinillo con EL GOLFANTE del manubrio.

LA SINI	No te hubiera reconocido. Aquí no es sitio para que hablemos.
EL GOLFANTE	¿Temes comprometerte?
LA SINI	La mujer en mi caso, con un amigo que nada le niega, está obligada a un miramiento que ni las casadas.
EL GOLFANTE	¿Que nada te niega? Quiere decirse que lo tienes todo con ese tío cabra.
LA SINI	Todo lo que se tiene con guita.
EL GOLFANTE	¿Que lo pasas al pelo?
LA SINI	Según se mire. Algo me falta, eso ya puedes comprenderlo. Tú has podido sacarme de la casa

DRINKS VENDOR	With plenty of wine and nicely seasoned… nice lean meat with no fat or gristle… I could just about be persuaded.
TASTELESS	His thoughts exactly.
DRINKS VENDOR	I doubt it!
MENACE	Well they say it wasn't just a one-off. They say he made a real feast of it! They're gathering the evidence against him… any day now he'll be out on his ear!
DRINKS VENDOR	That slippery eel! For as long as he sleazes out his daughter to the Commander the nets will be empty.
TASTELESS	Take the daughter to bed and put the trial to bed!
PRETTY-BOY	That's what you call high stakes! What a player!
DRINKS VENDOR	The soldiers aren't getting their wages, it's a den of vice and women are farmed like livestock.
PRETTY-BOY	Who's the lucky farmer?[7] Can I get a piece of the action?
DRINKS VENDOR	Get married, then put your missus up for auction.
PRETTY-BOY	What if she goes cheap?
TASTELESS	The cheaper the better. Look at Sini, fluttering her eyelashes at that organ grinder!

SINIBALDA, wearing a frilly peignoir and a petticoat, with bows on her shoes and a carnation in her hair, is chatting to the BUM over the garden gate.

SINI	I wouldn't have recognised you. This isn't a good place for us to talk.
BUM	Are you afraid he'll see you?
SINI	A woman in my position has to be extra careful. A generous bups is more jealous than a husband!
BUM	Does he give you everything you want?
SINI	Everything money can buy.
BUM	So you're happy as a pig in slop.
SINI	Depends what you mean. Something's obviously missing, that much you can see for yourself. You

de mi padre. ¿Que no tenías modo de vida? Pues atente a las consecuencias. ¿Lo tienes ahora? Pronta estoy a seguirte. ¡Ya te veo empalmado, pero no te lo digo por miedo! ¿Qué traes? ¡Un organillo! Vienes a camelarme con música. ¿Vas a sostenerme con escalas y arpegios? Mírame. No seas loco. ¡Y tienes toda la vitola de un golfante!

EL GOLFANTE	Tú dirás qué venga a ser sino un golfo, ciego por la mayor golfa, peleado con toda mi casta.
LA SINI	¡Cuándo asentarás la cabeza! ¿Dejaste los estudios? Pues has hecho mal. ¡Y tienes toda la vitola de un organillero! ¿Qué tiempo llevas dando al manubrio?
EL GOLFANTE	Tres meses. Desde que llegué.
LA SINI	¿Has venido siguiéndome?
EL GOLFANTE	Como te lo prometí.
LA SINI	Pero siempre pensé que no lo hicieses.
EL GOLFANTE	Ya lo ves.
LA SINI	¡Vaya un folletín!
EL GOLFANTE	Por ahí sacarás todo el mal que me has hecho.
LA SINI	Te has puesto pálido. ¿De verdad tanto ciegas por mí?
EL GOLFANTE	¡Para perderme!
LA SINI	Lo dices muy frío. No hay que hacerte caso. ¿Y que ventolera te ha entrado de ponerte a organillero?
EL GOLFANTE	Para el alpiste, y buscarte por las calles de Madrid. El lorito en tu ventana ha sido como un letrero.
LA SINI	¿Y qué intención traes? Empalmado lo estás. ¿Tú has venido con la intención de cortarme la cara?

winkled me out of my father's house, didn't you? I left you because you didn't have a penny to your name. But if you can keep me in the manner to which I've become accustomed, I'm all yours. You're giving me your murderous look, but I'm not just saying it because I'm afraid. What have you got there? An organ! Have you come to woo me with some pretty melodies?… You're not planning to keep me on scales and arpeggios, are you? Take a look at me! You must be out of your mind. And you've turned into such a miserable lowlife!

BUM   A miserable lowlife! What do you expect? My family's written me off, and I'm sick with love for the world's biggest slut!

SINI   You've never had your head screwed on properly! Have you given up your studies? That was silly of you. You even look like an organ grinder. How long have you been cranking away at that thing?

BUM   Three months now. Since I got here.

SINI   Did you come after me?

BUM   I promised I would.

SINI   It wasn't a promise I expected you to keep.

BUM   Well here I am.

SINI   How romantic!

BUM   Maybe now you'll understand what you've done.

SINI   You've turned pale! Are you really sick with love for me?

BUM   So sick I could die.

SINI   You say it very coldly. I don't think I can take you seriously. What gave you the crazy idea of becoming an organ grinder?

BUM   I needed to eat, and it meant I could wander the streets looking for you. That little parrot in your window was like a sign.

SINI   And what is it you want? You're looking murderous again. Have you come here to slash my face?

EL GOLFANTE	Al tío cebón es a quien tengo ganas de cortarle alguna cosa.
LA SINI	¿Qué mal te hizo? Con éste o con otro había de caer. Estaba para eso.
EL GOLFANTE	¡El amor que tienes por el lujo!
LA SINI	Tú nada podías ofrecerme. Pero con todo de no tener nada, de haber sido menos loco, por mi voluntad nunca hubiera dejado de verte. Te quise y te quiero. No seas loco. Apártate ahora.
EL GOLFANTE	¿Sin más?
LA SINI	¿Aquí qué más quieres?
EL GOLFANTE	Dame la mano.
LA SINI	¡Adiós, y que me recuerdes!
EL GOLFANTE	¿Vuelvo esta noche?
LA SINI	No sé.
EL GOLFANTE	¿Esperas al pachá?
LA SINI	Pero no se queda.
EL GOLFANTE	¿Cuál es tu ventana?
LA SINI	Te pones en aquella reja. Por allí te hablaré... Si puedo.

Huyóse LA SINI, *con bullebulle de almidones: Volvía la cabeza, guiñaba la pestaña: Sobre la escalinata se detuvo, sujetándose el clavel del pelo, sacó la lengua y se metió al adentro. El gachó del organillo, al arrimo de la verja, se ladea la gorra, estudiando la altura y disposición de las ventanas.*

| EL LORO | ¡Cubanita canela! |

BUM	It's that fat pig I'd like to slash; and I know just which bit I'd cut off too.
SINI	What's he ever done to you? If it hadn't been him it would have been somebody else. It was my time.
BUM	Gold digger!
SINI	You had nothing to offer me. But even so, if you hadn't been such a lunatic I'd have wanted to go on seeing you. I loved you and I love you still. Don't be a lunatic. Now get lost.
BUM	Is that it?
SINI	What more do you want?
BUM	Give me your hand.
SINI	Goodbye! Remember me!
BUM	Shall I come back tonight?
SINI	I don't know…
BUM	Is the Grand Turk due home?
SINI	Yes, but he won't be staying long.
BUM	Which is your window?
SINI	Wait by that railing. I'll talk to you there... if I can.

SINI runs off with a fussy rustling of her starched skirts. She turns her head, winking and fluttering at the organ grinder. She stops on the porch steps and pins the carnation more firmly into her hair, then sticks out her tongue and goes inside. The lovelorn BUM leans against the fence and pushes his cap back on his head, studying the height and position of the windows.

PARROT	Latin lovely!

ESCENA SEGUNDA

Lacas chinescas y caracoles marinos, conchas perleras, coquitos labrados, ramas de madrépora y coral, difunden en la sala nostalgias coloniales de islas opulentas: Sobre la consola y por las rinconeras vestidas con tapetillos de primor casero, eran faustos y fábulas del trópico. El loro dormita en su jaula abrigado con una manta vieja. A la mesa camilla le han puesto bragas verdes. Partida timbera. Donillea el naipe. Corre la pinta CHULETAS DE SARGENTO. *Hacen la partida seis camastrones. Entorchados y calvas, lucios cogotes, lucias manos con tumbagas, humo de vegueros, prestigian el último albur.* EL POLLO DE CARTAGENA, *viejales pisaverde, se santigua con una ficha de nacaradas luces.*

EL POLLO	¡Apré! Esto me queda.
EL CAPITÁN	¿Quiere usted cambio?
EL POLLO	Son cinco mil beatas.
EL CAPITÁN	A tanta devoción no llego. Puedo hacerle un préstamo.
EL POLLO	Gracias.
EL CAPITÁN	¿De dónde es la ficha?
EL POLLO	De Bellas Artes.
EL CAPITÁN	Puede usted disponer del asistente, si desea mandar a cambiarla. Si toma un coche, en media hora está de vuelta.
EL POLLO	Por esta noche me abstengo. Me voy a la última de Apolo. ¡Salud, caballeros!

Vinoso y risueño, con la bragueta desabrochada, levantó su corpulenta estampa el vencedor de Periquito Pérez: Saturnal y panzudo, veterano de toros y juergas, fumador de vegueros, siempre con luces alcohólicas en el campanario, marchoso, verboso, rijoso, abría los brazos el Pacha de LA SINIBALDA.

SCENE TWO

A room filled with burnished oriental figurines, sea conches, pearlescent shells, carved coconuts, branches of coral and madrepore. It has the nostalgically colonial air of an opulent isle. Set against the prim domestic cloths of the console and corner tables, the trinkets are exotically and ostentatiously tropical. The PARROT is dozing snugly in its cage, covered with an old blanket. The kitchen table[8] has been dressed in green breeches. Deep play.[9] CAPTAIN CUTLETS the Butcher has his trump card in hand. There are six bilkers at the table: silver and gold braid, bald patches, white hands glittering with rings. Smooth white necks. Cigar smoke. Sleights of hand as the game approaches its climax. The SPRING CHICKEN, as camp as he is old, crosses himself with a gambling chip. It gleams with pearly light.

SPRING CHICKEN	I'm broke! This is all I've got left.
CAPTAIN	Value?
SPRING CHICKEN	Five thousand pesetas.
CAPTAIN	Five thousand my foot. Next you'll be telling me you can feed the five thousand. The best I can do is to offer you a loan.
SPRING CHICKEN	Thanks.
CAPTAIN	Where's the chip from?
SPRING CHICKEN	Fine Arts.
CAPTAIN	We can send somebody to cash it for you if you like. If he takes a carriage he'll be back in half an hour.
SPRING CHICKEN	I'll bow out for tonight. I'm going to catch the late show at the Apollo.[10] Goodnight, gentlemen!

Crapulous and contented, his fly undone, the glorious GENERAL lifts his corpulent bulk out of the chair. He is an illustrious veteran, supremo of the minor skirmish and suppressor of the folk hero;[11] swarthy, big-bellied, an aficionado of bullfights and binges, a smoker of rough cigars. Alcoholic lights shine permanently from the belfry. Vigorous, garrulous, bellicose, SINIBALDA's pasha[12] opens his arms wide.

EL GENERAL	Pollo, vas a convidarnos.
EL POLLO	No hay inconveniente.
EL GENERAL	Chuletas, tira las tres últimas.
EL CAPITÁN	¡Ha cambiado el corte!
EL GENERAL	Me es inverosímil, Chuletas. Peina ese naipe. ¡Tú te las arreglas siempre para tirar la descargada!
EL CAPITÁN	¡Mi General, esa broma!
EL GENERAL	Rectificaré cuando gane.
EL CAPITÁN	Caballeros, hagan juego.

El vencedor de Periquito Pérez se colgó el espadín, se puso el ros de medio lado, se ajustó la pelliza y recorrió la sala marcándose un tango: Bufo y marchoso, saca la lengua, guiña del ojo y mata la bicha a estilo de negro cubano. LA SINIBALDA, por detrás de un cortinillo, asoma los ojos colérica, y descubre la mano con una lezna zapatera, dispuesta a clavarle el nalgario. Detuvo el brazo de la enojada EL POLLO DE CARTAGENA. EL GENERAL, asornado, vuelve a la mesa de juego, y el viejales pisaverde, en la puerta, templa con arrumacos y sermón los ímpetus de LA SINI.

EL POLLO	¡Vamos, niña, que estamos pasando un rato agradable entre amigos! Las diferencias que podáis tener, os las arregláis cuando estéis solos.
LA SINI	Don Joselito, me aburre un tío tan ganso. ¿Dónde ha visto usted peor pata?
EL POLLO	¡Niña!
LA SINI	Si se lo digo en su cochina cara. Y además está convencido de que lo siento. ¿Ha perdido?
EL POLLO	Ya puedes comprender que no me entretuve siguiendo su juego.
LA SINI	Ha perdido y se ha consolado como de costumbre.
EL POLLO	Yo me hubiera consolado mejor contigo.
LA SINI	Usted, sí, porque es un hombre de gusto y muy galante. ¿Ha perdido?
EL POLLO	No sé.
LA SINI	Ha perdido, y se ha puesto una trúpita para consolarse.
EL POLLO	Vendría de fuera con ella, y será anterior al proyecto de cometer el crimen.

GENERAL	Spring Chicken, you're buying us dinner.
SPRING CHICKEN	It would be my pleasure, General.
GENERAL	Deal the last three cards, Cutlets.
CAPTAIN	Somebody's shuffled the pack!
GENERAL	I couldn't care less. Shuffle them again. You always magically get rid of your worst cards in any case.
CAPTAIN	General, sir, you don't mean it!
GENERAL	If I win for once I'll take it back.
CAPTAIN	Let's play on, gentlemen.

The illustrious victor fixes his dress sword to his belt, twists his peaked cap to one side, buttons up his military jacket and marks a tango around the room. Animated and jovial, he sticks out his tongue, winks, and gyrates on the spot. SINIBALDA peeps out angrily from behind a curtain; she is wielding a shoe, the heel of which she prepares to bore into his rotating backside. The SPRING CHICKEN grabs her by the arm. The wry GENERAL returns to the card table; in the doorway, his foppish minder clucks and coos at SINI, attempting to divert her from her vicious plans.

SPRING CHICKEN	Come on, Sini, we're having a nice time between friends. I don't know what your beef is, but sort it out when you're alone.
SINI	I'm sick to death of him, Don José. Trust my luck to get landed with a stupid clown!
SPRING CHICKEN	Sini!
SINI	I'll say it to his fat face. And he's convinced I give a damn! Did he lose?
SPRING CHICKEN	I wasn't exactly watching his every move, you understand.
SINI	Don't tell me, he lost and then he drowned his sorrows the way he always does.
SPRING CHICKEN	I would have drowned them with you.
SINI	Yes, *you* would, because you're a man of taste and know how to treat a lady. Did he lose?
SPRING CHICKEN	I don't know.
SINI	He lost. Consolation comes bottled.
SPRING CHICKEN	I think he was already half-cut when he got here. Before he committed the crime.

LA SINI	¿Qué crimen?
EL POLLO	Una broma. Se ha consolado de la pérdida antes de la pérdida.
LA SINI	¿Y a qué ha dicho usted crimen?
EL POLLO	Un texto del Código Penal. Erudición que uno tiene.
LA SINI	¡Vaya texto! ¿Y usted se lo sabe por sopas el Código?
EL POLLO	Como el Credo.
LA SINI	¿Y dirá usted que se lo sabe?
EL POLLO	¿El Código?
LA SINI	El Credo.
EL POLLO	Para un caso de apuro.
LA SINI	Parece usted pariente de aquel otro que estando encaminándole preguntaba si eran de confianza los Santos Olios.
EL POLLO	Ése era mi abuelo.
LA SINI	Con su permiso, Don José.
EL POLLO	¡Sini, ten cabeza!

Brillos de cerillas, humo de vegueros. Los camastrones dejan la partida. Las cartas del último albur quedan sobre la mesa con un tuerto visaje. LA MUCAMA mandinga, delantal rayado, chancletas de charol, lipuda sonrisa, penetra en la sala y misteriosa toca la dorada bocamanga dEL GENERAL.

LA MUCAMA	Este papelito que horitita lo lea, Ño General.
EL GENERAL	Lo leeré cuando me parezca.
LA MUCAMA	Me ha dicho que horita y que me dé respuesta vuecencia.
EL GENERAL	Retírate y no me jorobes. Pollo, hágame usted el favor de quedarse. Le retengo a usted como peón de brega.

Se despedían los otros pelmazos. Eran cuatro: Un ricacho donostiarra, un famoso empresario de frontones, un cabezudo ex MINISTRO sagastino, y un catalán trapisondista, taurófilo y gran escopeta en las partidas de Su Majestad.

SINI	What crime?
SPRING CHICKEN	Just a little joke. He consoled himself for his loss before losing.
SINI	Why did you say it was a crime?
SPRING CHICKEN	Just quoting the Penal Code. Surprising what one stores away.
SINI	Get you! Don't tell me you know the Code off by heart.
SPRING CHICKEN	I can recite it like the Catholic Creed.
SINI	You can recite it?
SPRING CHICKEN	The Code?
SINI	The Creed.
SPRING CHICKEN	I could rustle it up in an emergency.
SINI	You must be related to that bloke, you know, the one who asked the priest on his way out if the holy oils were the real deal!
SPRING CHICKEN	That was my grandfather.
SINI	Excuse me, Don José.
SPRING CHICKEN	Sini, be sensible!

The flaring of matches, the smoke of cigars. The hustlers leave the game unfinished. The undealt cards lie on the table in a one-eyed grimace. The Mandinka MAID, wearing a striped apron, leather sandals and a plump smile, enters the room and enigmatically touches the GENERAL's golden cuff.

MAID	Excuse me, Mr General Sir, somebody deliver this note for you.
GENERAL	I'll read it later.
MAID	Sorry, sir, but they tell me you must read it now-now.
GENERAL	Go away and stop pestering me. Spring Chicken: stay if you don't mind. I'm retaining you as my foot soldier.

The remaining farts take their leave. There are four of them: a wealthy BASQUE CON MAN; a famous architectural impresario;[13] *an EX-MINISTER with a head like a bull; and MR RUMPUS the scheming Catalan Banker, aficionado of the bullfight and esteemed guest at His Majesty's shooting parties.*

EL TRAPISONDAS	¿Esa cena para cuándo, Don José?
EL POLLO	Ustedes dirán.
EL EX MINISTRO	Creo que no debe aplazarse.
EL TONGUISTA	Cena en puerta, agua en espuerta.
EL POLLO	Ustedes tienen la palabra.
EL TRAPISONDAS	Esta noche, en lo de Morán.
EL POLLO	¿Hace, caballeros?
EL TONGUISTA	¡Al pelo!
EL EX MINISTRO	¡Naturaca!
EL TRAPISONDAS	¡Evident!

Sale LA SINI. CHULETAS, recomiéndose, cuenta las fichas y las distribuye por los registros chinescos de la caja. – Pagodas, mandarines, áureos parasoles. – EL ASISTENTE, en brazado, saca abrigos, bastones, sombreros: Los reparte a tuertas, soñoliento, estúpido, pelado al cero. CHULETAS DE SARGENTO cierra la caja de fichas y naipes y, colocándosela bajo el brazo, se mete por una puerta oscura.

LA SINI	¿Le sería a usted muy molesto oírme una palabra, General?
EL GENERAL	Sini, no me hagas una escena. Sé mirada.
LA SINI	¡Vea usted de quedarse!
EL GENERAL	Es intolerable esa actitud.
LA SINI	Don Joselito, si a usted no le importan las vidas ajenas, ahueque.
EL POLLO	Obedezco a las damas. ¡Que haya paz!

EL POLLO DE CARTAGENA se tercia la capa a la torera y saluda marchoso en los límites de la puerta.

EL GENERAL	Pollo, si quedo con vida, caeré por casa de Morán.
LA SINI	¡Gorrista!
EL GENERAL	No me alcanzan tus ofensas.
EL POLLO	Si hay reconciliación, como espero, llévese usted a la niña.
EL GENERAL	Sini, ya lo estás oyendo. Échate un abrigo y aplaza la bronca.
LA SINI	Eso quisieras.

RUMPUS	When's this dinner of yours, Don José?
SPRING CHICKEN	Whenever suits.
EX-MINISTER	The sooner the better.
BASQUE CON MAN	Early birds, nice fat worms![14]
SPRING CHICKEN	I leave it to you to decide.
RUMPUS	Tonight, at Moran's place.
SPRING CHICKEN	How does that sound, gentlemen?
BASQUE CON MAN	Corking!
EX-MINISTER	Cracking!
RUMPUS	Capital!

SINI appears. CUTLETS resentfully counts up the chips and arranges them in the compartments of a Chinese box: pagodas, Mandarins, golden parasols. The shaven-headed ASSISTANT loads himself up with overcoats, hats and canes: sleepily, stupidly, he distributes them willy-nilly. CAPTAIN CUTLETS shuts the box full of cards and chips and, placing it under his arm, disappears through a dark doorway.

SINI	General, would you be so kind as to let me speak with you for a moment?
GENERAL	Sini, don't make a scene. Be sensible.
SINI	I think you should stay in!
GENERAL	You're being intolerable.
SINI	Don José, mind your own business and clear off.
SPRING CHICKEN	A lady's wish is my command. Anything to keep the peace!

The SPRING CHICKEN draws his cloak across his chest like a bullfighter and gives a flamboyant salute from the doorway.

GENERAL	If I'm still alive in half an hour I'll see you at Moran's.
SINI	Parasite!
GENERAL	I am deaf to your insults.
SPRING CHICKEN	If you can kiss and make up, and I sincerely hope you will, perhaps Sini could come along too.
GENERAL	Sini, you heard the man. Get your coat and stop being difficult.
SINI	Just to please you, I suppose.

EL POLLO	Mano izquierda, mi General.
EL GENERAL	Ésta quiere verme hacer la jarra.
LA SINI	¡Miserable!

EL POLLO DE CARTAGENA toma el olivo con espantada torera. EL GENERAL se cruza de brazos con heroico alarde y ensaya una sonrisa despreciando a la sinibalda.

EL GENERAL	Me quedo, pero serás razonable.
LA SINI	¿Has perdido?
EL GENERAL	Hasta la palabra.
LA SINI	Ésa nunca la has tenido.
EL GENERAL	El uso de la lengua.
LA SINI	¡Marrano!
EL GENERAL	Ya sacaste las uñas. Deja que me vaya.
LA SINI	¿Irte? Toma asiento y pide algo. ¡Irte! Será después de habernos explicado.
EL GENERAL	Tomo asiento. Y no hables muy alto.
LA SINI	No será por escrúpulo de que oiga mi padre. Tú y él sois dos canallas. Me habéis perdido.

EL CAPITÁN entra despacio y avanza con los dientes apretados, la mano en perfil, levantada.

EL CAPITÁN	No te consiento juicios sobre la conducta de tu padre.
LA SINI	¿Cuándo has tenido para mí entrañas de padre? Mira lo que haces. Harta estoy de malos tratos. Si la mano dejas caer, me tiro a rodar. ¡Ya para lo que falta!
EL GENERAL	Sinibaldo, aquí estás sobrando.
EL CAPITÁN	Tiene esa víbora mucho veneno.
LA SINI	Las hieles que me has hecho tragar.
EL CAPITÁN	Vas a escupirlas todas.
LA VOZ DEL POLLO	¡Socorro!

SPRING CHICKEN	Easy does it, General.
GENERAL	She's only interested in the contents of my pockets.
SINI	Miserable bastard!

The SPRING CHICKEN beats a hasty retreat. The GENERAL crosses his arms with heroic ostentation; his face splits into a scornful smile.

GENERAL	I'll stay, but you've got to be reasonable.
SINI	Did you lose?
GENERAL	Everything, including my good name.[15]
SINI	You never had a good name.
GENERAL	Let's go to bed and you can call me names.
SINI	Filthy pig!
GENERAL	Put those claws away and let me go out.
SINI	Go out? Why don't you just sit down and have another drink? Go out! Maybe once we've had a little chat.
GENERAL	Sit down. And lower your voice.
SINI	Don't tell me you're worried my father will hear us. You've both got your snouts in the trough and if I'm damned to hell it'll be your fault!

The CAPTAIN enters slowly and walks forward with his teeth clenched, his hand raised as if to strike her.

CAPTAIN	How dare you cast aspersions on your father!
SINI	When have you ever been a father to me? Look at you. I'm sick of being treated like this. If you touch me I'll throw myself on the floor. For all the good it'll do!
GENERAL	Captain, we don't need you here.
CAPTAIN	She's a poisonous snake.
SINI	It's all the bile I've had to swallow because of you.
CAPTAIN	I'll make you spit it out!
VOICE OF THE SPRING CHICKEN	Help!

*El eco angustiado de aquel grito paraliza el gesto de las tres figuras,
suspende su acción: Quedan aprisionadas en una desgarradura lívida
del tiempo, que alarga el instante y lo colma de dramática incertidumbre.
LA SINI rechina los dientes. Se rompe el encanto. EL CAPITÁN CHULETAS,
con brusca resolución, toma una luz y sale. EL GENERAL le sigue con
sobresalto taurino. En el marco de la ventana vestida de luna, sobre el
fondo estrellado de la noche, aparece EL GOLFANTE del organillo.*

EL GOLFANTE	¡Ya está despachado!
LA SINI	¡Mal sabes lo que has hecho! Darle pasaporte a Don Joselito.
EL GOLFANTE	¿Al Pollo?
LA SINI	¡A ese desgraciado!
EL GOLFANTE	¡Vaya una sombra negra!
LA SINI	¡Por obrar ciego! ¡Ya ves lo que sacas! ¡Meterte en presidio cargado con la muerte de un infeliz!
EL GOLFANTE	¡Ya no tiene remedio!
LA SINI	¿Y ahora?
EL GOLFANTE	Tu anuncio... ¡El presidio!
LA SINI	¿Qué piensas hacer?
EL GOLFANTE	¡Entregarme!
LA SINI	¡Poco ánimo es el tuyo!
EL GOLFANTE	Me ha enfriado el planchazo.
LA SINI	Pues no te entregues. Espérame. Ahora me voy contigo.

The anguished echo of this cry paralyses the expression on the three figures' faces. Their movement is suspended. They are trapped; time has been ripped open in a livid gash; the moment is prolonged and overflows with dramatic uncertainty. SINI grinds her teeth; the spell is broken. With brusque resolution, CAPTAIN CUTLETS reaches for a lamp and goes out. The GENERAL starts after him, cantering out of the room like a bull. Framed in the moonlit window against the starry backdrop of the night sky, the organ-grinding BUM appears.

BUM	I've blipped him at last!
SINI	You don't know what you've done! You've shanked Don José!
BUM	The Spring Chicken?
SINI	Poor bastard!
BUM	This is bad news.
SINI	You idiot! You see what happens when you don't use your eyes! You'll end up in chokey charged with murdering an innocent bystander!
BUM	What's done is done.
SINI	So what now?
BUM	Like you said… caboose!
SINI	What are you going to do?
BUM	Turn myself in.
SINI	Don't give up so easily!
BUM	I can't believe I made such a mess of it! It's given me the shakes.
SINI	Don't turn yourself in. Wait for me there. I'll come with you.

ESCENA TERCERA

Una puerta abierta: Fondo de jardinillo lunero: El rodar de un coche: El rechinar de una cancela: El glogloteo de un odre que se vierte: Pasos que bajan la escalera. CHULETAS DE SARGENTO *levanta un quinqué y aparece caído de costado Don Joselito.* EL CAPITÁN *inclina la luz sobre el charco de sangre, que extiende por el mosaico catalán una mancha negra. Se ilumina el vestíbulo con rotario aleteo de sombras: La cigüeña disecada, la sombrilla japonesa, las mecedoras de bambú. Sobre un plano de pared, diluidos, fugaces resplandores de un cuadro con todas las condecoraciones del* CAPITÁN. – *Placas, medallas, cruces.* – *Al movimiento de la luz todo se desbarata.* CHULETAS DE SARGENTO *posa el quinqué en el tercer escalón, inclinándose sobre el busto yacente, que vierte la sangre por un tajo profundo que tiene en el cuello.* EL GENERAL, *por detrás de la luz, está suspenso.*

EL CAPITÁN	No parece que el asesino se haya ensañado mucho. Con el primer viaje ha tenido bastante para enfriar a este amigo desventurado. ¡Y la cartera la tiene encima! Esto ha sido algún odio.
EL GENERAL	Está intacto. No le falta ni el alfiler de corbata.
EL CAPITÁN	Pues será que le mataron por una venganza.
EL GENERAL	Habrá que dar parte.
EL CAPITÁN	Dar parte trae consigo la explotación del crimen por los periódicos... ¡Y en verano, con censura y cerrada la Plazuela de las Cortes!... Mi General, saldríamos todos en solfa.
EL GENERAL	Es una aberración este régimen. ¡La Prensa en todas partes respeta la vida privada, menos en España! ¡La honra de una familia en la pluma de un grajo!
EL CAPITÁN	Sería lo más atinente desprenderse del fiambre y borrar el rastro.
EL GENERAL	¿Cómo?
EL CAPITÁN	Facturándolo.
EL GENERAL	¡Chuletas, no es ocasión de bromas!

SCENE THREE

An open door; a moonlit garden in the background; the sound of a coach rolling past; the creaking of an iron gate; wine glugging from a wineskin; footsteps coming down the stairs. CAPTAIN CUTLETS *holds up an oil lamp and shines it on Don José, who is lying on his side. He brings the light closer to the pool of blood, spreading a dark stain over the Catalan mosaic tiles. Shadows flutter and turn about the illuminated hall: a stuffed stork, a Japanese parasol, bamboo rocking chairs. The blurred outline of a frame glimmers fleetingly against the wall, briefly displaying the* CAPTAIN's *military decorations: plaques, medals, crosses. Everything disintegrates in the shifting light.* CUTLETS *places the oil lamp on the third step, leaning over the recumbent figure; blood oozes from a deep wound in his neck. The* GENERAL, *positioned behind the lamp, stands stock-still.*

CAPTAIN	This was done in cold blood. The murderer could have finished the job in one stroke, if all he wanted was to send our poor friend to the other side. He hasn't even taken his wallet! This was hatred, pure and simple.
GENERAL	He's intact. Not even his tiepin is out of place.
CAPTAIN	It must have been revenge.
GENERAL	We'll have to inform the authorities.
CAPTAIN	If we inform the authorities the newspapers will get hold of it… And in the summer, when the censors are at work and Parliament's shut up shop![16] General, we'd look ridiculous.
GENERAL	This regime is a disgrace. What happened to the privacy of the individual? It's respected everywhere but in Spain! The honour of a whole family spilled into an ink press!
CAPTAIN	The most sensible thing would be to get rid of the corpse and pretend it never happened.
GENERAL	How?
CAPTAIN	By sending it on a little trip.
GENERAL	Cutlets, this is no time for jokes!

EL CAPITÁN	Mi General, propongo un expediente muy aceptado en Norteamérica.
EL GENERAL	¿Y enterrarlo en el jardín?
EL CAPITÁN	Saldrán todos los vecinos con luces. Para eso mandas imprimir esquelas.
EL GENERAL	¿Y en el sótano?
EL CAPITÁN	Mi General, para los gustos del finado nada mejor que tomarle un billete de turismo. Lo inmediato es bajarlo al sótano y lavar la sangre. Vamos a encajonarle.
EL GENERAL	¿Persistes en la machada de facturarlo?
EL CAPITÁN	Aquí es un compromiso muy grande para todos, mi General. ¡Para todos!
EL GENERAL	¡Qué marrajo eres, Chuletas! Vamos a bajar el cadáver al sótano. Ya se verá lo que se hace.
EL CAPITÁN	El trámite más expedito es facturarlo, a estilo de Norteamérica.
EL GENERAL	¡Y siempre en deuda con el extranjero!
EL CAPITÁN	Si usted prefiere lo nacional, lo nacional es dárselo a la tropa en un rancho extraordinario, como hizo mi antiguo compañero el Capitán Sánchez.

LA SINI, aciclonada, bajaba la escalera con un lío de ropa atado en cuatro puntas, revolante el velillo trotero.

| LA SINI | ¡Infeliz! ¡Qué escarnio de vida! Me llevo una muda... Mandaré por el baúl... Aún no sé dónde voy. ¡Qué escarnio de vida! Mandaré un día de estos... |
| EL CAPITÁN | Con un puntapié vas a subir y meterte en tu alcoba, grandísima maula. Mi General, permítame darle un zarandazo de los pelos. ¡No la acoja! Hay que ser con este ganado muy terne. Si se desmanda, romperle la cuerna. |

CAPTAIN	General, I'm suggesting a measure widely accepted in North America.
GENERAL	Why not just bury it in the garden?
CAPTAIN	We'll have all the neighbours coming to see what's going on. If that's what you want we might as well strike up the funeral band.
GENERAL	Let's leave it in the cellar then.
CAPTAIN	General, the deceased would far rather go on a little holiday. The first thing we've got to do is take him down to the cellar and get rid of the blood. We're going to box him up.
GENERAL	You're not going to check him in like a bit of luggage!
CAPTAIN	This is a delicate situation for us all, General. For us all!
GENERAL	You're a clever chap, Cutlets! Let's take the corpse down to the cellar. Then we can decide what's best.
CAPTAIN	The most expedient course of action is to bag him up and check him in, as they do in North America.
GENERAL	You're always so taken with foreigners!
CAPTAIN	If you prefer a more home grown approach, we could take it to a soldiers' mess in the middle of nowhere and let the rank and file have their way with it.[17]

SINI rushes down the stairs like a cyclone. She is carrying a bundle of clothes, knotted hastily into a rough piece of flapping gauze.[18]

SINI	Poor bastard! What a pathetic life! I'll take a change of clothes with me… I'll send for my trunk… I don't know where I'm going yet. What a pathetic life! I'll send for it in a few days…
CAPTAIN	I'm going to kick you back up those stairs to your room, you useless bitch. General, allow me to slap some sense into her. Don't be kind to her! Be tough! Break her spirit! And if she disobeys, have her whipped!

LA SINI	¡Qué desvarío! Si mi papá se hace el cargo, puesta la niña en el caso de pedir socorro, alguno iba a enterarse.
EL CAPITÁN	¡Víbora!

LA SINI saca un hombro con desprecio y se arrodilla a un lado del muerto por la cabecera, sobre el fondo nocturno de grillos y luciérnagas. EL GENERAL y EL CAPITÁN cabildean bajo la sombrilla japonesa.

EL GENERAL	Sinibaldo, hay que ser prudentes. Si quiere irse, que se vaya. La Dirección de Seguridad se encargará de buscarla. Ahora no es posible una escena de nervios. ¡Sinibaldo, prudencia! Una escena de nervios nos perdería. Yo asumo el mando en Jefe.
LA SINI	¡Don Joselito, he de rezarle mucho por el alma! Me llevo su cartera, que ya no le hace falta. No iban esos marrajos a enterrarle con ella. ¡Qué va! ¡Pues que se remedie la Sini!
EL CAPITÁN	¡Mi, General, no puede consentirse que esa insensata se fugue del domicilio paterno con una cartera de valores!
EL GENERAL	Mañana se recupera. ¡Sería nuestra ruina una escena de nervios!
LA SINI	Las alhajitas tampoco las precisa. ¡Qué va! Don Joselito, he de rezarle mucho por el alma. Adiós, Don Joselito. ¡No sé si voy manchada de sangre!
EL CAPITÁN	Mi General, imposible para el honor de un padre tolerar esta pendonada.
LA SINI	¡Suéltame, Chuletas de Sargento!
EL CAPITÁN	Te ahogo, si levantas la voz.
LA SINI	¡Asesino! ¡Chuletas de Sargento!
EL GENERAL	¿Sinibaldo, qué haces? ¡Otro crimen!
EL CAPITÁN	¡Hija malvada!
LA SINI	¡Hija de Chuletas de Sargento!
EL GENERAL	Sini, no te desboques. Las paredes son de cartón. Todo se oye fuera. Sini, que el asistente te haga

SINI	Are you mad? If you whip me I'll have to cry for help, and somebody will hear me!
CAPTAIN	Snake!

SINI shrugs her shoulders with contempt and kneels by the dead man's head, silhouetted against a nocturnal backdrop of crickets and fireflies. The GENERAL and the CAPTAIN confer under the Japanese parasol.

GENERAL	Captain, we must be prudent. If she wants to go, we can't stop her. The police will pick her up. We can't have histrionics now. We must be prudent, Captain! A scene would be our undoing! I'm pulling rank on this issue.
SINI	Don José, I'll pray for your soul! I'm taking your wallet, now that you have no use for it. We don't want to let those sharks get hold of it, do we? No we don't! So just you let Sini take care of it!
CAPTAIN	General, as the father of this maniac, I cannot allow her to rashly defect with a valuable wallet!
GENERAL	We'll get it back tomorrow. A scene must be avoided at all costs!
SINI	You won't be needing your jewellery either, Don José. No you won't! Goodbye, Don José! I'll pray for your soul! I hope there's no blood on my hands!
CAPTAIN	General, it offends my honour as a father to have to tolerate this disgraceful behaviour.
SINI	Let go of me, Butcher!
CAPTAIN	Raise your voice and I'll strangle you.
SINI	Murderer! Butcher! Cannibal!
GENERAL	Captain, what are you doing? We'll have another crime on our hands!
CAPTAIN	Daughter from hell!
SINI	Daughter of the Butcher!
GENERAL	Sini, calm down. The walls are paper-thin. Everything can be heard from outside. Sini, let the maid make you a cup of herbal tea. You're

una taza de tila. Tienes afectados los nervios. No faltes a tu padre. Sini, no hagas que me avergüence de quererte.

LA SINI   ¡Abur y divertirse! Si algún guinda se acerca para detenerme, tened seguro que todo lo canto. Voy libre. La Sini se ha fugado al extranjero con Don Joselito. ¡Abur, repito!

EL CAPITÁN   ¡Las hay maulas! ¡Esa correspondencia tienes para tu padre, grandísimo pendón!

very upset. Don't shame your father. Sini, don't make me ashamed of loving you.

SINI
Bye-bye, have fun! And by the way, if a cop happens to arrest me, I'll sing like a canary! I'm setting myself free. Sini has run off to foreign parts with Don José. So bye-bye, my lovelies!

CAPTAIN
Women can be such bitches! Is that all you have to say to your father, you whore?

ESCENA CUARTA

Una rinconada en el café Universal: Espejos, mesas de mármol, rojos divanes. Mampara clandestina. Parejas amarteladas. En torno de un velador, rancho y bullanga, sombrerotes y zamarras: Tiazos del ruedo manchego, meleros, cereros, tratantes en granos. Una señora pensionista y un capellán castrense se saludan de mesa a mesa. Un señorito y un pirante maricuela se recriminan bajo la mirada comprensiva del MOZO, *prócer, calvo, gran nariz, noble empaque eclesiástico. LA SINIBALDA, con mantón de flecos y rasgados andares, penetra en el humo, entre alegres y salaces requiebros de la parroquia. Se acoge al rincón más oscuro y llama al* MOZO *con palmas.*

LA SINI	¡Café!
EL MOZO	¿Solo?
LA SINI	Con gotas.
EL MOZO	Si usted quiere cambiar de mesa, me queda otra libre en el turno. Aquí, con la corriente de la puerta, estará usted mal a gusto.
LA SINI	¡Qué va! Con el calorazo que hace, la corriente se agradece.
EL MOZO	Pues hay quien manda parar el ventilador. ¡Vaaa!

Llamaban de una peña marchosa. −Toreros, concejales, camelistas y pelmas.− EL MOZO se acercó con majestad eclesiástica y estuvo algunos instantes atento a las chuscadas de los flamencos. Siempre entonado y macareno, luego de limpiar el mármol, se salió del corro para poner el servicio de café en la mesa de LA SINI.

EL MOZO	Le ha caído usted en gracia al Manene. Me ha llamado porque disputaban sobre quién usted sea. Les ha caído usted en gracia, y la quieren sacar por un retrato que enseñó en la mesa un parroquiano. ¿No será usted la misma?
LA SINI	No, señor. Yo soy muy fea para retratarme. ¿Pero cuándo van a dejar de mirarme esos pelmazos?
EL MOZO	Están de broma.

SCENE FOUR

A corner of the Universal café: mirrors, marble-topped tables, red divans.
A discreetly positioned screen. Entwined couples. Riotous merrymaking
around a small table, at which a group in peasants' garb is eating:[20]
cheesemakers from La Mancha; honey sellers; wax-chandlers; grain
dealers. A lady lodger and an army priest nod at one another across their
respective tables. A young gentleman and a poof are having an argument;
a WAITER looks on sympathetically. SINIBALDA, in a tasselled shawl, slips
slyly through the smoke, to an accompaniment of parishioners' cat calls.
She finds the darkest corner of the room and summons the waiter with a
sharp clap.

SINI	Coffee, please!
WAITER	Black?
SINI	Stick a few drops in it, would you?
WAITER	That table there will be free in a moment, if you want to move. It's a bit draughty here.
SINI	No, it's fine! It's so hot, I don't mind the draught.
WAITER	Everybody else is asking for the fan to be turned off. Just coming!

A lively crowd of bullfighters, councillors, gamblers and louts is calling
the WAITER over to their table. He approaches them with ecclesiastical
majesty and stands listening for a moment to their cocky jibes. With
haughty pride he wipes down the marble tabletop, then leaves them to
bring SINI her coffee.

WAITER	That character over there likes the look of you. They called me over to see if I knew you. They're quite taken with you. It seems one of our regulars brought in a picture of a girl that looks just like you. Is it you?
SINI	No chance. I'm too ugly for anyone to take a picture of me. I wish those idiots would stop looking at me.
WAITER	They're just messing about.

LA SINI	¡Como si en su vida hubieran visto una mujer!
EL MOZO	¡Qué no estará usted acostumbrada a que la miren!
LA SINI	¡Asquerosos! Me parece que van a reírse de su mamasita.
EL MOZO	No es para que usted se incomode. Son gente alegre pero que no falta. Están en que usted es la del retrato. ¡Verá usted qué jarro de agua fría cuando los desengañe el Pollo de Cartagena!
LA SINI	¿Es el parroquiano?
EL MOZO	Contada la tarde que falta.
LA SINI	A ver si asoma y concluye el choteo de esos puntos. Estoy esperando a un amigo que tiene la sangre muy caliente.
EL MOZO	No habrá caso. Verá usted qué ducha cuando llegue el Pollo...
LA SINI	¿Y si ese sujeto hace novillos?
EL MOZO	Combina de mucho pote había de tener para faltar esta tarde. ¡Raro que siendo usted una hembra tan de buten, no la haya seguido alguna vez por esas calles!
LA SINI	¿Y sacado la fotografía? El punto ése, verá usted que por darse importancia, esta tarde no viene.
EL MOZO	Aún no es su hora.
LA SINI	Me gustaría conocerle.
EL MOZO	Pues fijamente hoy no falta. Casual que al irse anoche mandaba al botones a cambiarle una ficha de cinco mil beatas en la caja del Círculo. Fue motivado que viendo el atortolo del chico, que es novato, mudase de idea, y me pidió sesenta duros, cuyamente me prestó un parroquiano. ¿Qué mozo tiene hoy sesenta duros? ¡Eso otros tiempos!

SINI	You'd think they'd never seen a woman before!
WAITER	Don't tell me you're not used to the attention!
SINI	Filthy animals! They're only laughing because they're tight.
WAITER	Don't let it upset you. They like to have a bit of fun, that's all. They're convinced you're the girl in the picture. Just wait and see the look on their faces when the Spring Chicken tells them it's not you!
SINI	Is he the regular?
WAITER	He comes in every afternoon without fail.
SINI	Well let's see if he turns up and wipes the smile off their faces. I'm waiting for a very hot-tempered friend.
WAITER	Don't worry. They'll settle down when the Chicken arrives…
SINI	And what if he stands them up?
WAITER	It would have to be something big to stop him coming today. It wouldn't surprise me if he'd followed you, with your looks.
SINI	And taken a photograph? I bet he won't turn up this afternoon, just to keep them guessing.
WAITER	He normally comes in a bit later.
SINI	I'd like to meet him.
WAITER	He'll definitely be in today. It just so happens that last night, as he was leaving, he was going to send the errand boy to cash a chip for five thousand pesetas. But then he changed his mind when he saw how nervous the lad was: he's very young and inexperienced. So he asked me for sixty *duros*,[20] which I asked one of the regulars to lend me. How many waiters do you know with sixty *duros*? Maybe in the good old days…

Entran el andoba del organillo y un vejete muy pulcro, vestido de negro:
Afeminados ademanes pedagógicos, una afectada condescendencia de
dómine escolástico: El peluquín, los anteojos, el pañuelo que lleva a
la garganta y le oculta el blanco de la camisa como un alzacuello, le
inflingen un carácter santurrón y sospechoso de mandadero de monjas:
Le dicen EL SASTRE PENELA. *En voz baja conversan con* LA SINI. EL
GOLFANTE *le muestra una fotografía entre cínico y amurriado.*

EL GOLFANTE	El retrato de un pingo en camisa. ¡Mira si te reconoces! En la cartera del interfecto ha sido exhumado.
LA SINI	¡Se lo ha dado el canalla, sinvergüenza!
EL GOLFANTE	Trabajaba el endoso.
LA SINI	Anduvo un mes encaprichado por sacarme esa fotografía. ¡El aprecio que hizo el asqueroso! Entre unos y otros me habéis puesto en el pie de perderme. ¡Ya nada se me da! Hoy contigo... Mañana se acabó el conquis, a ganarlo para los dos con mi cuerpo. ¿Cómo estará de parné la cartera?
EL GOLFANTE	¡Limpia! Este amigo me ha dado una ayuda muy superior para desmontar la pedrería del alfiler y los solitarios. Como que el hombre se maneja sin herramientas. ¡Es un águila! En nueve mil melopeas pignoramos el lote, en la calle de la Montera. Por cierto que voy a quemar la papeleta.
EL SASTRE	¡Aquí no! ¡Prudencia! Pasa al evacuatorio.
EL GOLFANTE	En la cartera había documentos que en unas buenas manos son sacadineros. Dos pagarés de veinte mil pesetas con la firma del Pachá Bum-Bum. Una carta del propio invicto sujeto solicitando demoras, y una ficha de juego.
LA SINI	De Bellas Artes. ¡Cinco mil del alma! Dámela, que hay que cobrarla, y a no tardar.
EL GOLFANTE	¿Cómo se cobra?
LA SINI	Presentándose en caja.

Enter the organ-grinding BUM *and a very elegant old man dressed in black. He has the manner of an effeminate pedagogue, the affected condescension of a schoolmaster. He wears a toupee, spectacles, and a kerchief around his neck that looks like a dog collar: they give him the sanctimonious and suspicious air of a convent errand boy. He is known as the* TAILOR. *The two men talk to* SINI *in low voices. The organ grinder shows her a photograph with a mixture of cynicism and sadness.*

BUM	A picture of a tart in her nightie. Recognise her by any chance? They dug it out of the murdered man's wallet.
SINI	That bastard gave it to you! Shame on him!
BUM	He signed it over to me.
SINI	The old letch badgered me for a month to let him take that picture. He fancied me something rotten! If I'm damned to hell it won't be my fault! I don't care about anything anymore! Today I'm here with you… tomorrow we'll be back to square one and I'll be selling my body for the both of us. How much cash was there in the wallet?
BUM	None! My friend here has been a great help in taking the diamonds and the stone out of his brooch. You'd think the man had magic fingers. He's a genius! We pawned the lot for nine thousand *pesetas*![21] I'm burning the receipt, no question!
TAILOR	Not here! Be sensible! Let's retire to the gents.
BUM	There were papers in the wallet that in the right hands could be a real money-spinner. Two IOUs for twenty thousand pesetas, signed by Mister Pasha Boom-Boom; a letter from said glorious personage asking for an extension to his loan; and a gambling chip.
SINI	A chip from Fine Arts! Five thousand pesetas, come to my arms! Give it to me; I'll cash it.
BUM	How?
SINI	At the desk.

EL GOLFANTE	¡Es un paso comprometido!
LA SINI	¡Cinco mil beatas no son para dejarlas en el aire!
EL GOLFANTE	¡Conforme! Los documentos, estoy a vueltas... Hacerlos desaparecer es quemar un cheque al portador.
EL SASTRE	Hay que operar con mucho quinqué. Los presentas tú al cobro, y te ponen a la sombra: Se requieren otras circunstancias. Los que actúan en esos negocios son sujetos con muy buenas relaciones, que visitan los Ministerios. ¡El Batuco, que estos tiempos ha dado los mejores golpes, tiene padrinos hasta en la Gran Peña! Una masonería como la de los sarasas. El Batuco ha puesto a modo de una Agencia: ¡Una oficina en toda regla! Si queréis entenderos con él, fijamente está en los billares.
EL GOLFANTE	¿No será venderse?
EL SASTRE	Vosotros lo pensáis y aluego resolvéis. El Batuco vive de esas operaciones y su crédito está en portarse con decencia. Conoce como nadie el compromiso de ciertos negocios y puede daros una luz. Hoy todo lo hace la organización. ¡Vierais la oficina, montada con teléfono y máquina de escribir!... ¡Propiamente una Agencia!
EL GOLFANTE	¡Mira, Penela, que la mucha gente es buena en las procesiones!
EL SASTRE	Para sacarle lo suyo a esos papeles, hace falta el organismo de una Agencia. ¡Son otros horizontes! ¡Ahí tienes las contratas del ramo de Guerra! Para ti, cero, ni pensar en ello. ¡Para un organismo, ponerse las botas! Es su función propia... Ahora, si vosotros tenéis otro pensamiento...
LA SINI	¡Tan incentiva pintura los sentidos me enajena! ¡Suba usted por el Batuco!

BUM	It's a bit risky!
SINI	You're not going to let five thousand big ones slip through your fingers!
BUM	No, I'm not! And those papers are as good as banknotes: I won't be getting rid of those either!
TAILOR	You must proceed with great caution. If you try and cash them you'll get yourselves locked up. There is another way. There are people who take an interest in these situations, people with friends in high places, very high, government ministers no less... now take Dandy, for example: I don't know a more talented gentleman; he even has friends at the Gran Peña![22] A masonic organization if ever there was one. They're like a bunch of poofs. Dandy has set up an agency of sorts: a proper office, completely legit! If you want to talk to him, he's playing billiards as we speak.
BUM	Won't he rip us off?
TAILOR:	Think carefully. Make an informed decision. Dandy makes his living out of deals of this sort and they say he's a fair man. If anybody knows how sensitive certain business deals can be, he does. He might just be able to give you a bit of guidance. His organization will see to everything. You should see his office, all set up with a telephone and a typewriter and everything! A proper agency!
BUM	Listen, Tailor, people always know how to play to an audience!
TAILOR	If you want to make the most of those papers, you need an agency to help you. You've got to think big! You've a set of military contracts in your hands! If you go it alone, forget it: you'll get nothing. But if you go with an organisation, *kerching*! That's what it's there for... Now, if you've got a better idea...
SINI	Who will not change a raven for a dove?[23] Go and get Mr Dandyman!

EL GOLFANTE	¿Se puede uno confiar?
EL SASTRE	Hombre, yo siempre le he visto proceder como un caballero, y el asunto vuestro es un caso corriente.
EL GOLFANTE	Pues a no tardar.
EL SASTRE	Míralo, que baja de los billares. Don Arsenio, media palabra.

EL BATUCO accede, saludando con el puro: Chato, renegrido, brisas de perfumería y anillos de jugador, caña de nudos, bombín, botas amarillas con primores: Un jastialote tosco, con hechura de picador.

EL BATUCO	¿Qué cuenta el amigo Penela?
EL SASTRE	Estaba con una pata en el aire para remontarme en su busca y captura. Me había comprometido a relacionarle con esta interesante pareja. Tienen algunos documentos que desean negociar: Cartas y pagarés de un personaje. ¿Qué dice usted?
EL BATUCO	Acaso se pudiera intentar alguna travesura. ¡No sé! Sin conocer el asunto es imposible aventurar una opinión... Hay que estudiarlo. ¿Quién es el personaje?
EL SASTRE	Un heroico Príncipe de la Milicia.
EL BATUCO	¿Con mando?
EL SASTRE	Con mando.
EL BATUCO	¿Quién negocia los papeles?
EL SASTRE	Esta joven e inexperta pareja. Paseando, se han encontrado una cartera.
EL BATUCO	El propietario habrá dado parte a la Poli. Esos documentos de crédito en nuestras manos son papeles mojados.
LA SINI	El propietario no ha dado parte.
EL BATUCO	¿Seguro?
LA SINI	Tomó el tren para un viaje que será largo, y a última hora le faltó el tiempo hasta para las despedidas.
EL BATUCO	Entendido. ¿Pueden verse los documentos?
EL GOLFANTE	¡Naturaca!

BUM	Can we trust him?
TAILOR	I've only ever known him behave like a perfect gentleman, and he's seen cases like yours a thousand times.
BUM	Well let's get on with it.
TAILOR	Here he is, coming from the billiard table. Sir, a word if I may…

DANDY consents, waving to the TAILOR with his cigar. He is dwarfish and dark, perfumed and beringed; he carries a bamboo cane and wears a bowler hat and polished yellow boots. He is a coarse roughneck built like a picador.

DANDY	What's up, old boy?
TAILOR	I've been lurking here in the great hope that I would find you and catch you. I promised these charming people that I would introduce you to them. They have some papers that might be of interest to you and they would like to do business… letters and IOUs from a person of note. Can we interest you?
DANDY	We might be able to have a little fun with them. I really don't know. Without knowing the details it's impossible to say… I'll have to take a closer look. Who is this person of note?
TAILOR	A heroic Prince of the Celestial Army.[24]
DANDY	High ranking?
TAILOR	High ranking.
DANDY	Who's got the papers?
TAILOR	This pair of inexperienced young novices. They stumbled on a wallet.
DANDY	The owner must have reported it to the rozzers. These IOUs are no good to us.
SINI	The owner hasn't reported it.
DANDY	Are you sure?
SINI	He's gone on a long train journey. He didn't even have time to say goodbye.
DANDY	I see. May I see the papers?
BUM	Be my guest!

EL GOLFANTE saca del pecho un legajillo sujeto con una goma. EL BATUCO,
disimulado, hace el ojeo: Se detiene sobre una carta, silabea reticente.

EL BATUCO	«La rubiales se alegrará de verle, Chuletas de Sargento cantará guajiras y tirará el pego».
LA SINI	El viaje del andoba saltó impensadamente.
EL BATUCO	¿Muy largo, ha dicho usted?
LA SINI	Para una temporada.
EL BATUCO	¡Hablemos claro! ¡Esta carta es un lazo, una encerrona manifiesta! ¿Quién ha taladrado el billete al viajero? ¿No lo saben ustedes?
LA SINI	Le dio un aire al quinqué y se apagó para no verlo.
EL BATUCO	¡Como siempre! Y algún vivales se adelantó a tomar la cartera. ¿He dado en el clavo?
LA SINI	Ve usted más que un astrónomo. Usted debe predecir el tiempo.
EL BATUCO	Me alegro de no haberme equivocado. Es caso para estudiarse y meditarse. De gran mamporí si se sabe encauzar. Yo trabajo en una esfera más modesta. El negocio que ustedes traen es de los de Prensa y Parlamento. Yo soy un maleta, pero tengo buenas relaciones. Don Alfredo Toledano, el Director de El Constitucional me aprecia y puedo hablarle. Verá el asunto, que es un águila, y de los primeros espadas. Un hombre tan travieso puede con una campaña. En manos de un hombre de pluma estos papeles son un río de oro, en las nuestras un compromiso. Ése es mi dictamen. Con la amenaza de una campaña de Información periodística se puede sacar buena tajada. ¡Don Alfredo chanela como nadie la marcha de estos negocios! Cuando la repatriación, formó una

The BUM takes a bundle of papers, loosely secured with an elastic band, from his inside pocket. DANDY riffles through them with affected nonchalance. He pauses over one of the letters and reads it aloud with difficulty.

DANDY	'Blondie will be pleased to see you, Cutlets will sing Cuban folksongs[25] and cheat at cards as usual.'
SINI	He left rather sooner than expected.
DANDY	He's gone on a long journey, you say?
SINI	Longish.
DANDY	Let's not beat around the bush! This letter is a snare, a trap! Anyone can see that. Who drilled the ticket into the passenger? You must know!
SINI	The wind blew out the light so I couldn't see.
DANDY	Surprise, surprise! And some clever dick came out of nowhere and stole the wallet. Is that about the size of it?
SINI	You see more than an astronomer. You should give weather forecasts.
DANDY	I'm so glad I've understood. I'll certainly consider it; yes… quite an opportunity, if only we can catch the tigger by its toe! I generally work in a more modest sphere. This business belongs to the Press and to Parliament. I'm nobody special, but I do have friends in high places. The editor of *El Constitucional*[26] is a friend of mine and I can speak freely with him. He'll understand the situation: he's a genius, and a leader of men. Such a wise and subtle man as he can threaten to start a campaign. For a man armed with a pen, these papers are a river of gold. For us, they are a danger. That is my opinion. But with the threat of a newspaper campaign we might get something out of it. The editor *savvy* better than anyone how this kind of business is done! When the soldiers were sent home from Cuba, he set up a charity.

Sociedad. ¡Un organismo de lo más genial, para la explotación de altos empleados! Si ustedes están conformes, me pondré al habla con el maestro.

LA SINI   ¡A no dejarlo!

EL GOLFANTE   ¿Dónde nos avistamos?

EL BATUCO   Aquí. ¿Hace?

EL SASTRE   Entiendo que aquí ya nos hemos lucido bastante. En todas las circunstancias de la vida conviene andarse con quinqué...

EL BATUCO   Pues pasen ustedes por la Agencia. Pez, 31.

LA SINI   ¡A ver si hacemos changa!

EL BATUCO   ¡Seguramente! Huyo veloz como la corza herida.

EL SASTRE   ¡Orégano sea!

EL GOLFANTE   Sinibalda.

LA SINI   ¿Qué se ofrece?

EL GOLFANTE   ¿Y de la ficha, qué?

LA SINI   ¡Cobrarla!

EL GOLFANTE   ¿Estás en ello?

LA SINI   ¡Naturaca!

EL GOLFANTE   En tus manos la dejo. Yo me najo para cambiar de vitola en El Águila.

	A wonderful organisation, devoted entirely to the needs of high-ranking officers![27] If you agree, I'll speak to the master.
SINI	There's no time to lose!
BUM	Where shall we meet?
DANDY	Here. Agreed?
TAILOR	I think we've outdone ourselves. But it's always wise to go carefully…
DANDY	I'll look forward to seeing you at the Agency, then.
SINI	Let's hope we can do a deal.
DANDY	I'm sure we can! I make haste like a hart or a roe!
TAILOR	Over spice-scented hills may you go![28]
BUM	Sinibalda.
SINI	You rang?
BUM	What about the chip?
SINI	Let's cash it!
BUM	Are you up for it?
SINI	You bet!
BUM	I'll leave it with you. Next stop: swanky threads.[29]

ESCENA QUINTA

Un mirador en el Círculo de Bellas Artes, Tumbados en mecedoras, luciendo los calcetines, fuman y bostezan tres señores socios: Un viejales CAMASTRÓN, *un goma* QUITOLIS *y* EL CHULAPO AYUDANTE *en el tapete verde.– Se oye la gresca del billar, el restallo de los tacos, las súbitas aclamaciones. El viejales* CAMASTRÓN, *con los lentes de oro en la punta de la nariz, repasa los periódicos. Filo de la acera encienden sus faroles los simones. Pasa la calle el campaneo de los tranvías y el alarido de los* PREGONES.

PREGONES	*¡Constitucional! ¡Constitucional! ¡Constitucional! ¡Clamor de la Noche! ¡Corres! ¡Heraldo! ¡El Constitucional,* con los misterios de Madrid Moderno!
EL CAMASTRÓN	¡Cerrojazo de Cortes, crimen en puerta! ¡Señores, qué manera de hinchar el perro!
EL QUITOLIS	¿Cree usted una fantasía la información de El Constitucional?
EL CAMASTRÓN	Completamente. ¡La serpiente de mar que se almuerza a un bañista todos los veranos! ¡Las orgías de Madrid Moderno! ¿Ustedes creen en esas saturnales con surtido de rubias y morenas?
EL CHULAPO	No las llamemos saturnales, llamémoslas juergas. Ese antro de locura será alguna Villa-Laura o Villa-Ernestina.
EL CAMASTRÓN	¿Y ese personaje?
EL CHULAPO	Cualquiera. Uno de tantos beneméritos carcamales que le paga a la querida un hotel a plazos.
EL QUITOLIS	La información alude claramente a una ilustre figura, que ejerció altos mandos en Ultramar.
EL CHULAPO	¡Ultramar! Toda la baraja de Generales.
EL QUITOLIS	No lo será, pero quien tiene un apaño en Madrid Moderno...
EL CAMASTRÓN	¿Con una rubia? Es indispensable el agua oxigenada. Vea usted los epígrafes: «La rubia opulenta». ¿Corresponden las señas?

SCENE FIVE

An enclosed balcony at the Circle of Fine Arts. Three gentlemen are relaxing in their rocking chairs, smoking, yawning, and showing their socks. They are the DODGER, *the* DIVER *and the* LOUT OF THE GREEN BAIZE.[30] *The sounds of an argument at the billiard table – sudden shouts and swearing – can be heard in the background. The wizened* DODGER *peers at the newspaper through the gold-rimmed glasses perched on the end of his nose. Lined up against the pavement outside, cabs are lighting their lanterns. A tram bell clangs down the street, followed by the cries of a newspaper seller.*

SELLER	Read all about it! Mystery and Mayhem in Modern Madrid![31] Read all about it!
DODGER	Parliament closes its doors, and suddenly we're awash with criminals! Really, gentlemen, it's a lot of hot air.
DIVER	Do you think the hacks are making it up?
DODGER	Completely. The sea snake that swallows an innocent bather whole each Summer. The orgies of Modern Madrid, with an assorted cast of blondes and brunettes. It's a carnival parade! Don't tell me you're taken in.
LOUT	It's not exactly a carnival; it's more of a bender. The eye of the storm will be some suburban villa.
DODGER	And who is this character?
LOUT	Who cares? Another distinguished old codger who pays his beloved's nightly hotel bills.
DIVER	The report clearly mentions somebody important; he seems to have held high office in the colonies.
LOUT	The colonies! Pick a General, any General.
DIVER	I don't believe it. It'll just be somebody with a nice little set-up in the suburbs.
DODGER	Is there a blonde in this scenario? Hydrogen peroxide is quite essential to these stories. The headline is always the same: "A curvaceous blonde." Am I right?

EL QUITOLIS	Sí, señor, corresponden.
EL CAMASTRÓN	Pues ya sólo falta el nombre del tío cachondo para que decretemos su fusilamiento.
EL QUITOLIS	La alusión del periódico es diáfana.
EL CAMASTRÓN	¡Seré yo ciego!
EL CHULAPO	Yo creo que todos menos usted la hemos entendido.
EL CAMASTRÓN	Son ustedes unos linces.
EL CHULAPO	Y usted un camándulas. Usted sabe más de lo que dice El Constitucional.
EL CAMASTRÓN	Yo no sé nada. Oigo verdaderas aberraciones y me abstengo de darles crédito.
EL CHULAPO	Sin darles crédito y como tales hablillas, usted no está tan en la higuera. Usted guarda un notición estupendo. ¡Tiemble usted que se lo pueden escacharrar! Se le ha visto en muy buena compañía. ¡Una rubia opulenta!
EL CAMASTRÓN	Rubias opulentas hay muchas. La que yo saludé aquí esta tarde, sin duda lo es.
EL CHULAPO	Parece que a esa gachí le rinde las armas un invicto Marte.
EL CAMASTRÓN	¡Es usted arbitrario!
EL CHULAPO	¡La chachipé!
EL CAMASTRÓN	Y aun cuando así sea. ¿Qué consecuencias quiere usted deducir?
EL CHULAPO	Ninguna. Señalar coincidencias.
EL CAMASTRÓN	Muy malévolamente. Otros muchos en el caso de Agustín Miranda. Un solterón con una querida rubia. ¡Van ustedes demasiado lejos!

DIVER	Yes indeed, good sir, you are on the money.
DODGER	Now all we need is the name of the randy bugger so that we can order him to be shot.
DIVER	The newspaper report makes only vague allusions to his identity.
DODGER	I must be blind!
LOUT	It's plain as day!
DODGER	You are a pair of lynx.
LOUT	And you are a Pharisee. You know more than the newspaper.
DODGER	I know nothing. I hear lies of the worst kind and I refuse to pay them any heed.
LOUT	You may well pay them no heed! You may well claim it's all gossip, but you didn't come down in the last shower. You're sitting on a splendid bombshell. Are you afraid somebody will set it off for you? You've been seen in very good company. A curvaceous blonde, no less!
DODGER	There are plenty of curvaceous blondes to go round. The bit of skirt I spoke to this afternoon is certainly one of them.
LOUT	Well it appears your little bird has persuaded some indomitable war-god to surrender his arms.
DODGER	How fickle you are!
LOUT	The cap fits!
DODGER	And what if she has? What do you deduce from it?
LOUT	Nothing whatsoever. I'm simply pointing out a coincidence.
DODGER	With great malice. Many others are looking at General Miranda's case. An unmarried man with his beloved blonde. Wouldn't it rot your socks!

Se acerca un babieca fúnebre, alto, macilento: La nuez afirmativa, desnuda, impúdicamente despepitada, incrusta un movimiento de émbolo entre los foques del cuello: El lazo de la chalina, vejado, deshilachado, se abolla con murria de filósofo estoico, a lo largo de la pechera: La calva aparatosa con orla de melenas, las manos flacas, los dedos largos de organista, razonan su expresión anómala y como deformada, de músico fugado de una orquesta. Toda la figura diluye una melancolía de vals, chafada por el humo de los cafés, el roce de los divanes, las deudas con EL MOZO, las discusiones interminables.

EL BABIECA	¡La gran noticia!
EL CHULAPO	¡Ya se la escacharraron a Don Paco! No hay secreto. ¡Ya se la escacharraron!
EL BABIECA	¿Han leído ustedes la información de El Constitucional? ¿Saben ustedes cuáles son los nombres verdaderos?
EL CHULAPO	No es difícil ponerlos.
EL BABIECA	¿Saben ustedes que la rubia estuvo aquí esta tarde?
EL CHULAPO	Ya lo sabemos.
EL BABIECA	¿Y que cobró en la caja una ficha de cinco mil beatas?
EL QUITOLIS	¿Pago de servicios? Yo no estaba tan enterado. ¡Cinco mil del ala!...
EL BABIECA	Hay otra versión más truculenta.
EL CHULAPO	¡Olé!
EL BABIECA	¡Que le dieron pasaporte al Pollo de Cartagena!
EL CHULAPO	¿Don Joselito? ¡Si acabo de verle en los billares!
EL BABIECA	Imposible. Nadie le ha visto desde ayer tarde.
EL CHULAPO	¿Está usted seguro? ¿A quién, entonces, he saludado yo en los billares?
EL BABIECA	Don Joselito llevaba precisamente una ficha de cinco mil pesetas. La única que faltaba al hacer el recuento.
EL CHULAPO	¿Es la que cobró la rubia?
EL BABIECA	Indudablemente.

They are approached by the figure of the tall, gaunt, funereal BOZO. *His large and exposed Adam's apple, lodged like an embolism in his throat, moves with impertinent immodesty against his starched collar. The vexed, threadbare knot of his cravat puts up with the assault: hanging down the front of his shirt, it wears the gloomy air of a stoic philosopher. He has an extravagant bald patch, bristling with long hairs, and the thin, long-fingered hands of an organist, the perfect accompaniment to his anomalous and deformed expression: he looks like a musician that has escaped from the orchestra. His figure distils the melancholy mood of a waltz, a mood debased by smoky cafés, debts, divans, and interminable arguments.*

BOZO	Big news!
LOUT	Don Paco's bomb has already gone off! The secret's out. The bomb's gone off!
BOZO	Have you read the report in the newspaper? Do you know the names of those involved?
LOUT	It's not what I would call a brainteaser.
BOZO	Did you know the blonde was here this afternoon?
LOUT	We know.
BOZO	And did you know she cashed a chip for five thousand pesetas?
DIVER	Payment for services rendered? Now that's news to me. Five thousand, you say!
BOZO	There's a more shocking version of the story.
LOUT	Olé!
BOZO	They say they popped the Spring Chicken.
LOUT	Don José? I've just seen him playing billiards!
BOZO	Impossible. Nobody's seen him since yesterday afternoon.
LOUT	Are you sure? Who did I wave to at the billiard table then?
BOZO	Don José had a chip for exactly five thousand pesetas. It was the only one missing when they counted them up.
LOUT	And the blonde cashed it?
BOZO	No doubt about it.

EL CAMASTRÓN	¡Don Joselito estará con una trúpita!
EL QUITOLIS	Eso no se me había ocurrido.
EL CAMASTRÓN	*El Constitucional* le había sugestionado a usted la idea del crimen.
EL QUITOLIS	¡A ver si resulta todo ello una plancha periodística!
EL CAMASTRÓN	Verán ustedes cómo nadie exige responsabilidades.

Entra un chisgarabís: Frégoli, monóculo, abrigo al brazo, fuma afectadamente en pipa: Es meritorio en la redacción de El Diario Universal: El Conde de Romanones, para premiar sus buenos oficios, le ha conseguido una plaza de ama de leche en la Inclusa.

EL REPÓRTER	¡La gran bomba! Voy a telefonear a mi periódico. Se ha verificado un duelo en condiciones muy graves entre el General Miranda y Don Joselito Benegas.
EL CHULAPO	¿Por la rubia?
EL REPÓRTER	Eso se cuenta.
EL CAMASTRÓN	¿Usted nos dirá quién es el muerto? ¿Porque, seguramente, habrá un muerto? ¡Acaso dos!
EL REPÓRTER	¡No se atufe usted conmigo! Soy eco opaco de un rumor.
EL CAMASTRÓN	Acabe usted.
EL REPÓRTER	En la timba decían algunos que Don Joselito estaba agonizando en un hotel de Vicálvaro.
EL CAMASTRÓN	Ésos ya quieren llevarse el suceso al distrito de Canillejas. ¡Señores, no hay derecho! ¡Formemos la liga Pro Madrid Moderno! Afirmemos el folletín del hombre descuartizado y la rubia opulenta. ¡Ese duelo es una comedia casera! No admitamos esa ñoñez. El descuartizado y la rubia se nos hacen indispensables para pasar el verano.
EL CHULAPO	Bachiller, ¿qué dicen en teléfonos de la información de El Constitucional?

DODGER	He's just over the edge with the rams!
DIVER	I hadn't thought of that.
DODGER	The newspaper made you think a crime had been committed.
DIVER	Don't tell me some journalist's cooked it all up!
DODGER	Nobody will be called to account – you'll see!

Enter a sot, wearing a trilby hat and a monocle. He carries his coat over his arm and smokes his pipe with pompous affectation. He is an unpaid apprentice at the editorial offices of El Diario Universal: to reward him for his good work, the newspaper's influential owner[32] has found him a position as wet nurse at the foundling hospital.[33]

REPORTER	What a scoop! I'm going to telephone the newspaper. There are reports of a serious duel between General Miranda and Don José Benegas.
LOUT	Over the blonde?
REPORTER	So they say.
DODGER	Tell us who copped it! Somebody must have copped it! Maybe both of them copped it!
REPORTER	Don't harass me. I bring merely the distant echo of a rumour.
DODGER	Spit it out then.
REPORTER	The word at the card table is that Don José is dying in a little house on the outskirts of town.[34]
DODGER	These people are trying to shift all the attention out to some remote suburb![35] Gentlemen, they have no right! Let us form a league in defence of Modern Madrid! Let us stand up for the melodrama of the dismembered man and the curvaceous blonde. This duel is a trifling comedy! We cannot allow such inanity. We need dismemberment and blondes to get us through the Summer.
LOUT	So come on clever clogs,what's the word on the report in *El Constitucional*?

EL REPÓRTER	Para empezar, demasiado lanzada... De no resultar un éxito periodístico, pueden fácilmente tirarse una plancha... Sin embargo, algunos compañeros que han interrogado a los vecinos del hotel obtuvieron datos muy interesantes. Un vigilante de consumos asegura haber visto a la rubia, que escapaba con un gatera. Y son varios los vecinos que afirman haber oído voces pidiendo socorro.
EL CAMASTRÓN	¿Pero no sostenía a la rubia un Marte Ultramarino? Veo mucha laguna.
EL QUITOLIS	Indudablemente.
EL CHULAPO	¿Y se cree que haya habido encerrona?
EL REPÓRTER	Me abstengo de opinar... La maledicencia señala a un invicto Marte. Todo el barrio coincide en afirmarlo.
EL QUITOLIS	Allí habrá caído como una bomba la información de El Constitucional.
EL REPÓRTER	Allí saben mucho más de lo que cuenta el periódico.
EL CAMASTRÓN	¡El hombre descuartizado! ¡Se nos presenta un gran verano!

Irrumpe rodante y estruendosa la bola del mingo, y dos jugadores en mangas de camisa aparecen blandiendo los tacos: Vociferan, se increpan. Los PREGONES *callejeros llegan en ráfagas.*

PREGONES	*¡El Constitucional! ¡Constitucional! ¡Constitucional! ¡Clamor de la Noche! ¡Corres! ¡Heraldo! ¡El Constitucional,* con los misterios de Madrid Moderno!

REPORTER	If you ask me, they've put all their eggs in one basket... if it doesn't pull in the readers, they'll look a right bunch of charlies... Having said that, some colleagues of mine have been talking to the neighbours and they've been saying some very interesting things. A local tax collector[36] swears he saw the blonde lamming off with some geezer. And several people say they heard cries for help.
DODGER	But wasn't the blonde shacked up with a war-god from the exotic reaches of the former empire? I don't see the connection.
DIVER	Of course you don't.
DODGER	And they think it was a trap?
REPORTER	No comment. But people are pointing fingers at an indomitable Mars. The whole neighbourhood agrees.
DIVER	That newspaper report must have hit them like a bomb blast.
REPORTER	Those people know far more than the newspaper does.
DODGER	The Dismembered Man! We have a wonderful summer ahead of us!

A billiard ball rolls thunderously into the room. Two players appear in their shirtsleeves, swearing noisily and insulting one another. There are bursts of shouting from the street vendors below.

SELLER	Read all about it! Mystery and Mayhem in Modern Madrid!

ESCENA SEXTA

Un salón, con grandes cortinajes de terciopelo rojo, moldurones y doradas rimbombancias. Lujo oficial con cargo al presupuesto. Sobre una mesilla portátil, la botella de whisky, el sifón y dos copas. El Vencedor de Periquito Pérez, a medios pelos, en mangas de camisa, con pantalón de uniforme, fuma tumbado en una mecedora, y alterna algún requerimiento a la copa. Detrás, el ASISTENTE, inmóvil, sostiene por los hombros la guerrera de Su Excelencia. Asoma el CAPITÁN CHULETAS de SARGENTO.

EL CAPITÁN	¿Hay permiso, mi General?
EL GENERAL	Adelante.
EL CAPITÁN	¿Ha leído usted El Constitucional de esta noche? ¡Una infamia!
EL GENERAL	Un chantaje.
EL CAPITÁN	Si usted me autoriza, yo breo de una paliza al Director.
EL GENERAL	Sería aumentar el escándalo.
EL CAPITÁN	¿Y qué se hace?
EL GENERAL	Arrojarle un mendrugo. En estos casos no puede hacerse otra cosa... Las leyes nos dejan indefensos ante los ataques de esos grajos inadaptados. Necesitamos un diplomático y usted no lo es. ¡Chuletas, estoy convencido de que vamos al caos! Esta intromisión de la gacetilla en el privado de nuestros hogares es intolerable.
EL CAPITÁN	¡La protesta viva del honor militar se deja oír en todas partes!
EL GENERAL	Sinibaldo, saldremos al paso de esta acción deletérea. Las Cámaras y la Prensa son los dos focos de donde parte toda la insubordinación que aqueja, engañándole, al pueblo español. Siempre he sido enemigo de que los organismos armados actúen en política, sin embargo, en esta ocasión me siento impulsado a cambiar de propósito. Necesitamos un diplomático y usted no lo es. Toque usted el timbre. ¿Y el fiambre?

SCENE SIX

An ornate and gilded parlour of red velvet curtains and plaster mouldings: a benefit in kind, chargeable to the taxpayer. An occasional table with a bottle of whisky, a siphon and two glasses. The illustrious veteran, half soused and in his shirtsleeves, in uniform from the waist down, is reclining in a rocking chair and smoking; more pressing concerns are abrogated in favour of his tipple. Behind him, an AIDE-DE-CAMP *stands motionless, holding up His Excellency's military jacket by the shoulders.* CAPTAIN CUTLETS *the Butcher sticks his head round the door.*

CAPTAIN	General, may I?
GENERAL	Please, come in.
CAPTAIN	Have you read this evening's *Constitucional*? It's a disgrace!
GENERAL	It's blackmail.
CAPTAIN	With your permission, sir, I'll make sure the editor is black and blue by the morning.
GENERAL	We would simply be making things worse.
CAPTAIN	What are we to do, then?
GENERAL	Throw him a bone. In these situations it's all one can do... The law leaves us defenceless before the assaults of these maladjusted vultures. We need to be diplomatic, and that is not your strong suit. Cutlets, we are heading for total chaos, I know it! This invasion of the newsmongers into the privacy of our homes is intolerable!
CAPTAIN	Resounding protestations of military honour are everywhere to be heard!
GENERAL	We will face this deleterious accusation head on! Parliament and the Press are the twin breeding grounds of this insubordination, and they enfeeble the Spanish people by deceiving them. I have always been opposed to the participation of the armed forces in politics; however, on this occasion I feel obliged to change my view. We need a diplomat and you are not he. Ring the bell. What of the corpse?

EL CAPITÁN	Encajonado, pero sin decidirme a facturarlo.

Un oficial con divisas de AYUDANTE asomó rompiendo cortinas, y quedó al canto, las acharoladas botas en compás de cuarenta y cinco grados.

EL AYUDANTE	¡A la orden, mi General!
EL GENERAL	A Totó necesitaba. ¿Qué hace Totó?
EL AYUDANTE	Tomando café.
EL GENERAL	Dígale usted que se digne molestarse.
EL AYUDANTE	¿Eso no más, mi General?
EL GENERAL	Eso no más. Póngase usted al teléfono y pida comunicación con el Cuartel de San Gil. Que un momento a conferenciar conmigo el Coronel. Quedo esperando a Totó. Puede usted retirarse.
EL AYUDANTE	¡A la orden, mi General!
EL CAPITÁN	¡El fiambre en el sótano es un compromiso, mi General!
EL GENERAL	¡Y gordo!
EL CAPITÁN	¡Mi General, hay que decidirse, y montar a caballo!
EL GENERAL	Redactaré un manifiesto al país. ¡Me sacrificaré una vez más por la Patria, por la Religión y por la Monarquía! Las figuras ilustres del generalato y los jefes con mando de tropas, celebramos recientemente asamblea... Faltó mi aquiescencia: ¡Con ella ya se hubiera dado el golpe!
EL CAPITÁN	El golpe sólo puede darlo usted.
EL GENERAL	Naturalmente, yo soy el único que inspira confianza en las altas esferas. Allí saben que puedo ser un viva la Virgen, pero que soy un patriota y que sólo me mueve el amor a las Instituciones. Eso mismo de que soy un viva la Virgen prueba que no me guía la ambición, sino el amor a España. Yo sé que esa frase ha sido pronunciada por una Augusta Persona. ¡Un viva la Virgen, señora, va a salvar el Trono de San Fernando!

| CAPTAIN | Boxed up, but not yet checked in. |

An officer appears wearing his ADJUTANT's stripes. He pulls open the curtains and stands to attention, his patent leather boots at exactly forty-five degrees.

ADJUTANT	You called, sir!
GENERAL	It was Toto I wanted. What's Toto up to?
ADJUTANT	He's having a cup of coffee.
GENERAL	Ask him if he would be so kind as to leave his cup of coffee and come and see me.
ADJUTANT	Is that all, sir?
GENERAL	That's all. Get on the telephone and ask to be connected to the San Gil barracks. I would like to speak briefly to the Colonel. I'll wait here for Toto. You may go.
ADJUTANT	Yes, sir!
CAPTAIN	The corpse in the basement is rather compromising, General!
GENERAL	I am aware of that.
CAPTAIN	General, we must decide what to do, and do it fast!
GENERAL	I will address a manifesto to the people of Spain! I will once more sacrifice myself for the Motherland, for the Faith and for the Monarchy! The most illustrious and high-ranking officers and the chiefs of staff recently convened... and I dissented. Had I agreed, the coup would already have taken place!
CAPTAIN	Only you can stage a coup.
GENERAL	Naturally. Only I can inspire the confidence of the upper echelons. I'm a *bon viveur*, it is true, but nobody can question my patriotism, nor doubt that I am motivated by love for our Institutions. A *bon viveur*, no doubt; but this only proves that I am guided, not by ambition, but by my love of Spain. I know these words have been uttered by an August Personage.[37] This *bon viveur*, madam,[38] will save the Throne of Saint Ferdinand, patron saint of the Military and the Monarchy!

EL CAPITÁN	Mi General, usted, si se decide y lo hace, tendrá estatuas en cada plaza.
EL GENERAL	¡Me decido, Chuletas! ¡Estoy decidido! Pero no quiero perturbar la vida normal del país con una algarada revolucionaria. No montaré a caballo. Nada de pronunciamientos con sargentos que ascienden a capitanes. Una acción consciente y orgánica de los cuadros de Jefes. Que actúen los núcleos profesionales de la Milicia. ¡Hoy no puede contarse con el soldado ni con el pueblo!
EL CAPITÁN	¡El soldado y el pueblo están anarquizados!

TOTÓ aparece en la puerta: Rubio oralino, pecoso, menudo: Un dije escarlata con el uniforme de los Húsares de Pavía.

TOTÓ	¡A la orden, mi General!
EL GENERAL	Totó, vas a lucirte en una comisión. Ponte al teléfono y pide comunicación con el Director de *El Constitucional.* ¿Estás enterado del derrote que me tiran?
TOTÓ	Y no me explico lo que van buscando!... Si no es una paliza...
EL GENERAL	Dinero.
TOTÓ	Pero usted los llevará a los Tribunales. Un proceso por difamación.
EL GENERAL	¿Un proceso ahora, cuando medito la salvación de España? En estos momentos me debo por entero a la Patria. Tengo un deber religioso que cumplir. ¡La salud pública reclama un Directorio Militar! Mi vida futura está en ese naipe. Hay que acallar esa campaña insidiosa. Ponte al habla con el Director de El Constitucional. Invítale a que conferencie conmigo.
TOTÓ	El Brigadier Frontaura espera que usted le reciba, mi General.
EL GENERAL	Que pase.
TOTÓ	Mi Brigadier, puede usted pasar.

CAPTAIN	General, if you can be decisive, there will be a statue of you in every square.
GENERAL	I am being decisive, Cutlets! I have made a decision! But I don't want to disturb the normal life of the country with endless cries of revolution. I will not be seen on horseback. There will be no *coup d'état*; no promoting of sergeants to captains. It will be a conscious and organic action on the part of the Chiefs of Staff. The professional core of the Military must take charge. Neither the soldier nor the citizen can be counted upon these days!
CAPTAIN	The soldier and the citizen have become anarchists!

TOTO appears in the doorway: he is golden blonde, freckle-faced and slight. A small red stone glints against his uniform, which is of the Hussars' regiment of Pavia.[39]

TOTO	You wanted to see me, General!
GENERAL	Toto, I have a job for you. I have every confidence that you will do it well. Get on the telephone and ask to speak to the editor of *El Constitucional*. I take it you are you aware of the damaging allegations against me?
TOTO	I can't understand what they hope to get out of it! Other than a beating...!
GENERAL	Money.
TOTO	But you will take them to court. For libel!
GENERAL	A trial now, when I am planning the salvation of Spain? The times demand that I devote myself completely to the Motherland. I have a religious duty to fulfil. The health of our nation demands Military Governance! The cards have foretold it. We must silence this insidious campaign. Talk to the editor of *El Constitucional*. Invite him to speak with me.
TOTO	The Brigadier hopes you will receive him, General.
GENERAL	Let him in.
TOTO	Brigadier, you can come in.

EL BRIGADIER	¡He leído El Constitucional! ¡Supongo que necesitas padrinos para esa cucaracha!
EL GENERAL	Fede, yo no puedo batirme con un guiñapo. ¿Ladran por un mendrugo? ¡Se lo tiro!
EL BRIGADIER	¡Eres olímpico!
EL GENERAL	Aprovecho la ocasión para decirte que he renunciado mi empleo de pararrayos del actual Gobierno.
EL BRIGADIER	Algo sabía.
EL GENERAL	Pues eres el primero a quien comunico esta resolución.
EL BRIGADIER	Los acontecimientos están en el ambiente.
EL GENERAL	Si ha de salvarse el país, si no hemos de ser una colonia extranjera, es fatal que tome las riendas el Ejército.
EL BRIGADIER	No podías sustraerte. Me parece que más de una vez hemos discutido tu apoyo al actual Gobierno.
EL GENERAL	Pero yo no quiero dar el espectáculo de un pronunciamiento isabelino.

EL AYUDANTE asoma de nuevo entre cortinas, la mano levantada a los márgenes de la boca, las botas en ángulo.

EL AYUDANTE	Una Comisión de Jefes y Oficiales desea conferenciar con vuecencia.
EL GENERAL	¿Ha dicho usted una Comisión de Jefes y Oficiales? ¿Quién la preside?
EL AYUDANTE	El Coronel Camarasa.
EL GENERAL	¿Por qué Camarasa?
EL AYUDANTE	Acaso como más antiguo.
EL GENERAL	¿Viene sobre el pleito de recompensas?
EL AYUDANTE	Seguramente, no. Paco Prendes, a medias palabras, me dijo que la idea surgió al la información de El Constitucional. Se pensó en un desfile de Jefes y Oficiales. Luego se desistió, acordándose que sólo viniese una representación.

BRIGADIER	I have read *El Constitucional!* How do you plan to defend yourself against this insidious cockroach?
GENERAL	My friend, we must not cry over spilt milk. So they bark like dogs after a bone? Then let me throw them one!
BRIGADIER	You are quite Olympian!
GENERAL	Let me take this opportunity to inform you that I will no longer be a lightning conductor for the present Government.
BRIGADIER	Word had already reached me.
GENERAL	But you're the first person I've spoken to about it!
BRIGADIER	I felt it in my water.
GENERAL	If the country is to be saved, if we are not to be colonised by a foreign power, fate decrees that I take the reins of the Army.
BRIGADIER	It is a responsibility you cannot shirk! I believe we have discussed your support for the present Government on more than one occasion.
GENERAL	But I don't want people to think I've orchestrated a coup of the kind we've had in the past.[40]

The ADJUTANT makes another appearance from behind the curtains, his hand cupped around his mouth and his boots at right angles.

ADJUTANT	A Delegation of Chiefs and Officers wishes to meet with you, sir.
GENERAL	A Delegation of Chiefs and Officers? Who is in charge?
ADJUTANT	Colonel Camarasa.[41]
GENERAL	Why Camarasa?
ADJUTANT	Perhaps because he's the oldest.
GENERAL	Does he want to see me about the pay dispute?
ADJUTANT	I doubt it, sir. It seems they got the idea on reading the report in *El Constitucional*. They thought of organising a full parade of Chiefs and Officers. Then they decided against it, and agreed to send a representative party instead.

EL GENERAL	Hágalos usted pasar. Me conmueve profundamente este rasgo de la familia militar. ¡Mientras la honra de cada uno sea la honra de todos, seremos fuertes!

EL GENERAL se abrochaba la guerrera, se ajustaba el fajín, se miraba las uñas y la punta brillante de las botas. EL AYUDANTE, barbilindo, cuadrado, la mano en la sien, se incrustaba en un quicio de la puerta, dejando pasar a la Comisión. EL CORONEL CAMARASA, que venía al frente, era pequeño, bizco, con un gesto avisado y chato de faldero con lentes: Se le caían a cada momento.

EL CORONEL	Mi General, la familia militar ha visto con dolor, pero sin asombro, removerse la sentina de víboras y asestar su veneno sobre la honra inmaculada de Su Excelencia. Se quiere distraer al país con campañas de escándalo. Mi General, la familia militar llora con viriles lágrimas de fuego la mengua de la Patria. Un Príncipe de la Milicia no puede ser ultrajado, porque son uno mismo su honor y el de la Bandera. El Gobierno, que no ha ordenado la recogida de ese papelucho inmundo...
EL GENERAL	La ha ordenado, pero tarde, cuando se había agotado la tirada. No puede decirse que tenga mucho que agradecerle al Gobierno. ¡Si por ventura no es inspirador de esa campaña! El Presidente, con quien he conferenciado esta mañana, conocía mi resolución de dar un manifiesto al país. Entre ustedes, alguno sabe de este asunto tanto como yo. Señores, el Gobierno, calumniándome, cubriéndome de lodo, quiere anular el proyectado movimiento militar. Tengo que hablar con algunos elementos. Si los amigos son amigos, ésta será la última noche del Gobierno.
EL CORONEL	¡Mi General, mande usted ensillar el caballo!

GENERAL   Send them in! I am deeply moved by the
                 generosity of the military family. For as long as
                 one man's honour is every man's honour, we will
                 be strong!

The GENERAL *buttons up his jacket, adjusts his sash, and inspects his
nails and the shiny toes of his boots. The boyishly handsome* ADJUTANT
*squares his clean-shaven jaw, salutes, and stands to attention. He presses
himself into the doorframe to let the Delegation pass. The* COLONEL,
*at its head, is small, cross-eyed, and puggish; he wears the knowing
expression of a bespectacled lapdog. His glasses slip constantly down
the bridge of his snub nose.*

COLONEL   General, the military family has observed with
                 pain, though not with surprise, the stirring of
                 this nest of snakes and has noted the venomous
                 ejaculations aimed at Your Excellency's
                 untarnished honour. They want nothing more than
                 to amuse the country with scandalous campaigns.
                 General, the military family weeps hot, virile
                 tears for the decadence of our Motherland. A
                 Prince of the Army must not be insulted, because
                 his honour and the honour of the Flag are one and
                 the same thing. The Government, which has not
                 demanded the withdrawal of that disgusting rag...
GENERAL   It did order it, but too late, only after it had sold
                 out. I couldn't say that I have much to thank the
                 Government for. I wouldn't be surprised if it was
                 not responsible for the campaign! The President,
                 with whom I spoke this morning, knew of my
                 intention to declare my manifesto to the nation.
                 No doubt some of you know as much about this
                 situation as I. Gentlemen, the Government, by
                 defaming me, by slinging mud at me, wishes to
                 forestall a military uprising. There are individuals
                 with whom I must speak. If my friends are truly
                 my friends, tonight will be this Government's last!
COLONEL   General, order your horse to be saddled!

ESCENA ÚLTIMA

Una estación de ferrocarril: Sala de tercera. Sórdidas mugres. Un diván de gutapercha vomita el pelote del henchido. De un clavo cuelgan el quepis y la chaqueta galoneada de un empleado de la vía. Sórdido silencio turbado por estrépitos de carretillas y silbatadas, martillos y flejes. En un silo de sombra la pareja de dos bultos cuchichea. Son allí EL GOLFANTE *del organillo y la* SINIBALDA.

LA SINI	¡Dos horas de retraso! ¡Hay que verlo!
EL GOLFANTE	Presentaremos una demanda de daños a la Compañía.
LA SINI	¡Asadura!
EL GOLFANTE	¿Por qué no?
LA SINI	¡Te arrastra!
EL GOLFANTE	¡Dos horas dices!... ¡Pon cuatro!
LA SINI	¡Y eso se consiente!
EL GOLFANTE	¡Que acabarás por pedir el libro de reclamaciones!
LA SINI	¡Dale con la pelma! ¡Después de tantos afanes, que ahora nos echen el guante!... ¡Estaría bueno!
EL GOLFANTE	¡Y todo puede suceder!
LA SINI	¡Qué negras entrañas tienes!

Llegan de fuera marciales acordes. Una compañía de pistolos con bandera y música penetra en el andén. Un zanganote de blusa azul, quepis y alpargatas, abre las puertas de la sala de espera. EL CORONEL, *que viste de gala, con guantes blancos, obeso y ramplón, besa el anillo a un Señor* OBISPO. *Su Ilustrísima le bendice, agitanado y vistoso en el negro ruedo de sus familiares. Sonríe embobada la Comisión de Damas de la Cruz Roja. Pueblan el andén chisteras y levitas de personajes: Muchos manteos, fajines y bandas. Los repartidos corros promueven rumorosas mareas de encomio y plácemes. El humo de una locomotora que maniobra en agujas, infla todas las figuras alineadas al canto del andén, llena de aire los bélicos metales de figles y trombones, estremece platillos y bombos, despepita cornetines y clarinetes. Llega el tren Real.*

FINAL SCENE

A train station: a grimy third-class waiting room. A bloated rubber seat vomits its goat-hair stuffing onto the floor. The cap and braided jacket of a railway employee hang from a nail. There is a sordid silence, interrupted only by the din of wheelbarrows and train whistles, hammers and metal bindings. A shadowy pair whispers in a dark corner. They are the organ-grinding BUM and SINIBALDA.

SINI	A two-hour delay! Can you believe it!
BUM	I'm going to sue the Company for damages!
SINI	Settle down.
BUM	Why shouldn't I?
SINI	You'll give us away!
BUM	Two hours you say...! Make it four!
SINI	And people put up with it!
BUM	You'll end up making a complaint yourself.
SINI	God, you do go on! After everything we've been through, if they should catch us now...! That would be just our luck!
BUM	It could happen!
SINI	You're miserable to your rotten core!

The sound of martial chords from outside. A company of infantry soldiers marches onto the platform with its music and its flag. An oaf in a blue shirt, kepi and espadrilles opens the door to the waiting room. The COLONEL, wearing formal dress and white gloves, looks fat and coarse: he kisses the ring of the Reverend BISHOP. Eye-catching and gipsy-like in the black circle of his subordinates, His Excellency blesses him. A delegation of Red Cross Ladies smiles inanely. The platform is overwhelmed with the top hats and frock coats of important personages; mantles, sashes and stripes proliferate. Eddies of people bring murmuring tides of congratulation and praise. An engine is manoeuvring at a set of points. The billowing steam swells the line of figures at the edge of the platform, trumpets the bellicose metal of bugles and trombones, rattles cymbals and bass drums, whips up cornets and clarinets. The Royal train pulls in.

LA SINI	¡Si no pensé que todo este aparato era para nosotros!
EL GOLFANTE	Demasiada goma. Hay que hacerse cargo.
LA SINI	Ya me vi con esposas, entre bayonetas.
EL GOLFANTE	Menudo pisto que ibas a darte. Nada menos que una compañía con bandera. ¡Ni que fueses la Chata!
LA SINI	¡Pues no has estado tú sin canguelo!
EL GOLFANTE	¡Qué va!
LA SINI	Ver cómo perdías el rosicler fue lo que me ha sobresaltado.
EL GOLFANTE	¿Que perdí el color?
LA SINI	¡Y tanto!
EL GOLFANTE	¡Habrá sido a causa de mis ideas! Las pompas monárquicas son un agravio a la dignidad ciudadana.
LA SINI	¡Ahora sales con esa petenera!
EL GOLFANTE	¡Mis principios!
LA SINI	¡Y un jamón!
EL GOLFANTE	Vamos a verle la jeta al Monarca.

En el andén, una tarasca pechona y fondona, leía su discurso frente al vagón regio. Una DOÑA SIMPLICIA, Delegada del Club Fémina, Presidenta de las Señoras de San Vicente y de las Damas de la Cruz Roja, Hermana Mayor de las Beatas Catequistas de Orbaneja. La tarasca infla la pechuga buchona, resplandeciente de cruces y bandas, recoge el cordón de los lentes, tremola el fascículo de su discurso.

DOÑA SIMPLICIA	Señor: Las mujeres españolas nunca han sido ajenas a los dolores y angustias de la Patria. Somos hijas de Teresa de Jesús, María Pita, Agustina de Aragón y Mariana Pineda. Como ellas sentimos, e intérpretes de aquellos corazones acrisolados, no podemos menos de unirnos a la acción regeneradora iniciada por nuestro glorioso Ejército. ¡Un Príncipe de la Milicia levanta su espada victoriosa y sus luces

SINI	I didn't think this display was in our honour!
BUM	An orgy of silks and satins.[42] Would you believe it.
SINI	I had a vision of myself in handcuffs, between bayonets.
BUM	You think a lot of yourself. A company with a flag, no less. You're not the Princess Royal, you know![43]
SINI	Don't tell me your pants are clean!
BUM	Come off it!
SINI	It was watching the colour drain out of your face that scared me more than anything.
BUM	Did I go white?
SINI	As chalk!
BUM	I wasn't frightened; I was offended! Royal ceremonies are an affront to the dignity of citizens.
SINI	Please, spare me.
BUM	These are my principles we're talking about!
SINI	And I'm the Virgin Mary.
BUM	Let's see if we can't catch a glimpse of his Ugly Mugness.

On the platform, a fat old trout with a large bust is making a speech before the royal train. She is MRS SIMPLETON, representative of the Club Femina, President of the Women's Association of Saint Vincent and the Red Cross Ladies, and senior member of the Christian Sisters' Organization of Orbaneja. Her chest, puffed out like a pigeon's, is bedecked with crosses and ribbons. Gathering up the cord of her spectacles, she warbles the first instalment of her speech.

MRS SIMPLETON	Your Majesty: The women of Spain have never been insensible to the Nation's pain and anguish. We are daughters of the Spanish heroines[44] who have risen to defend it during times of trouble. We feel as they; with the same pureness of heart, we dutifully unite with our glorious Army in calling for regeneration! A Prince of the Celestial Army brandishes his sword of victory

inundan los corazones de las madres españolas! Nosotras, ángeles de los hogares, juntamos nuestras débiles voces al himno marcial de las Instituciones Militares. ¡Señor, en unánime coro os ofrecemos nuestras fervientes oraciones y los más cordiales impulsos de nuestras almas, fortalecidas por la bendición de la Iglesia, Madre Amantísima de Vuestra Dinastía! Como antaño el estudiante de las aulas salmantinas alfombraba con el roto manteo el paso de su dama, nosotras alfombramos vuestro paso con nuestros corazones. ¡Vuestros son, tomadlos! ¡Ungido por el derecho divino, simbolizáis y encarnáis toda las glorias patrias! ¿Cómo negaros nada, diga lo que quiera Calderón?

EL MONARCA, asomado por la ventanilla del vagón, contraía con una sonrisa belfona la carátula de unto, y picardeaba los ojos pardillos sobre la delegación de beatas catequistas. Aplaudió, campechano, el final del discurso, sacando la figura alombrigada y una voz de caña hueca.

EL MONARCA	Ilustrísimo Señor Obispo: Señoras y Señores: Las muestras de amor que en esta hora recibo de mi pueblo son, sin duda, la expresión del sentimiento nacional, fielmente recogido por mi Ejército. Tened confianza en vuestro Rey. ¡El antiguo Régimen es un fiambre, y los fiambres no resucitan!
VOCES	¡Viva el Rey! ¡Viva España! ¡Viva el Ejército!
SU ILUSTRÍSIMA	¡Viva el Rey Católico de España!
UNA BEATA	¡Católico y simpático!
DOÑA SIMPLICIA	¡Viva el Rey intelectual! ¡Muera el ateísmo universitario!
UN PATRIOTA	¡Viva el Rey con todos los atributos viriles!
EL PROFESOR DE HISTORIA	¡Viva el nieto de San Fernando!

and it casts a penetrating light into the hearts of Spanish mothers! We, the angels of the hearth, lift our frail voices to join the martial hymn of the Armed Forces. With one voice we offer you our most fervent prayers and our most respectful but heartfelt sentiments, fortified by the blessings of the Church, Most Loving Mother of Your Majesty's Dynasty! As a student, in days gone by, would have laid his torn cape at the feet of his beloved to ease her way, we lay our hearts at your feet to ease yours. They are yours: take them! Anointed by divine right, thou art both the symbol and incarnation of all glorious nations! How could we deny thee anything, whatever Calderón might say?[45]

The MONARCH, *leaning out of the window of the railway carriage, contracts the greasy mask of his face into a horse-lipped smile; his wide, loamy eyes flit playfully over the delegation of Christian Sisters. He breaks into genial applause at the end of the speech and wriggles his earthworm's body a little further out of the train. His voice, when he speaks, is like a hollow reed.*[46]

MONARCH	Reverend Bishop, Ladies and Gentlemen: the love you have shown us today is surely an expression of the nation's true sentiments, articulated by our loyal Army. Have faith in your King. The former regime is dead meat, and dead meat can't be brought back to life!
VOICES	Long live the King! Long live Spain! Long live the Army!
BISHOP	Long live the Catholic King of Spain!
DEVOUT LADY	A Catholic and a gentleman!
MRS SIMPLETON	Long live the spirit of the Monarchy! Down with the atheist universities!
A PATRIOT	Long live the King, a man amongst men!
TEACHER OF HISTORY	Long live the grandson of Saint Ferdinand!

| EL GOLFANTE | ¡Viva el regenerador de la sociedad! |
| LA SINI | ¡Don Joselito de mi vida, le rezaré por el alma! ¡Carajeta, si usted no la diña, la hubiera diñado la Madre Patria! ¡De risa me escacho! |

El tren Real dejaba el andén, despedido con salvas de aplausos y vítores. DOÑA SIMPLICIA derretíase recibiendo los plácemes del Señor Obispo. Un REPÓRTER metía la husma, solicitando las cuartillas del discurso para publicarlas en El Lábaro de Orbaneja.

BUM   Long live the saviour of society!
SINI   Don Joselito, my love, I'll pray for your soul!
             Christ, if you hadn't carked it the Motherland
             would have! It's so funny I could wet myself!

The royal train pulls away from the platform, to rounds of applause and huzzahs. MRS SIMPLETON melts like a pudding as she receives the congratulations of the BISHOP. A REPORTER sniffs around, trying to get a copy of her speech so he can publish it in the local rag.[47]

NOTES

1   'Una mucama mandinga' [A Mandinka Maid]: The word 'mucama' is an Americanism, whilst 'mandinga' [mandinka] refers to one of the largest ethnic groups in West Africa.

2   *Horchata* is a traditional drink typically made in Spain with tigernuts, water and sugar.

3   Madrid Moderno: See the introduction (pp. 22–23) for the significance of Valle-Inclán's frequent references to this part of the city.

4   According to Cardona and Zahareas, the 'jaunty favourite of the light opera' that was the *Marcha de Cádiz* traditionally accompanied the embarkation of soldiers destined for Cuba (1970, 200).

5   This is an allusion to the notorious 'crimen del capitán Sánchez' [the crime of Captain Sánchez], discussed in the introduction (p. 20).

6   The term 'mambí' is applied in Cuba to those who fought for independence against the Spanish forces in 1895–98.

7   There is a play on words here between the meaning in Spanish of 'rancho' as both 'farm' and '[soldiers'] mess'. The play uses the language of animal husbandry and other animal imagery to reinforce the brutality of the characters.

8   The 'mesa camilla,' emblematic of domestic life in Spain, is a round table with space underneath it for a heater.

9   'Deep play': in 18th century parlance, 'playing for high stakes' (Gay, *Beggar's Opera*, 101). Valle describes it as a 'partida timbera': the adjective 'timbera' seems to be a neologism based on the noun 'timba,' meaning a card game, a hand in a game of chance, or a low gambling house.

10 The Teatro Apolo was built between 1871 and 1873, financed by the banker Gargollo. Situated on the Calle de Alcalá, it was built on the site of the former convent of San Hermenegildo, which was disentailed in 1836 and demolished in 1870. The theatre, inaugurated in 1873, became one of the most emblematic theatres of the Restoration period, and was known as the 'cathedral of the *género chico*' or light opera. It was closed and bought up in 1929 by the Banco de Vizcaya, which subsequently demolished it in order to build its own headquarters.

11 'El vencedor de Periquito Pérez' [Suppressor of the folk hero]: Pedro Agustín Pérez ("Periquito") was a Cuban patriot and hero of the so-called 'guerra chiquita' [little war] (1879–80) which preceded the main conflict of the Cuban War of Independence (1895–1898). He was one of the initiators of the Cuban revolution against the Spanish, leading it in Guantánamo.

12 'Pachá' or pasha: A Turkish honorary title formerly conferred by the Sultan on officers of high rank, roughly equivalent to a knighthood. Valle-Inclán's use of the title contributes to the oriental and, by implication, decadent ambiance within which the military leader operates.

13 Possibly a figure intended to represent the impresarios responsible for the development of Madrid moderno, Julián Marín, Mariano Santos Pineda, and Francisco Navacerrada Sánchez.

14 'Cena en puerta, agua en espuerta'. As Senabre notes, Valle-Inclán appears to have

made up this saying, the meaning of which is rather obscure. According to the DRAE, 'en puerta' refers to the first card dealt after the pack is shuffled, whilst the plural 'en puertas', means 'about to occur'. An 'espuerta' is a woven basket, seemingly an inappropriate vessel for water, though it was sometimes used for catching and displaying fish. 'A espuertas' means 'in abundance': although this idiomatic phrase could imply that the Basque Con Man is looking forward to a hearty meal, I've assumed that Valle-Inclán meant to refer to the basket ('cena en puertas, agua a espuertas' would have rhymed and scanned just as well, if that was indeed what he intended to say). So I tentatively interpret that the saying means something along the lines that dinner should happen as soon as possible, because putting it off would be a missed opportunity (like a basket leaking water but containing no fish).

15 'Sini: Has perdido? Gen: Hasta la palabra. Sini: Esa nunca la has tenido. Gen: El uso de la lengua'. There is a series of puns in this exchange based around the word 'palabra' [word]. Sini asks the General if he has lost, to which he replies that he has lost even 'la palabra', *i.e.* the capacity to speak (because he is drunk). But 'palabra de hombre' also means to 'give one's word' and so 'palabra' can be broadly synonymous with honour. 'Tener la palabra' is also to have one's say. Here the idea that he has 'perdido la palabra' seems to suggest not only that he is too drunk to speak, but that he is letting Sini take control of the situation, and furthermore that he has been shamed by losing all his money at cards. The pun on 'palabra' is extended by the reference to 'lengua' [tongue/language] in the General's following line which, judging by Sini's response, is lewdly suggestive.

16 'Cerrada la Plazuela de las Cortes' [Parliament's shut up shop]: The Plaza de las Cortes is home to the Palacio de las Cortes, or Spanish Parliament building. The reference (repeated in scene 5) to Parliament's closure is confusing, since the coup has not yet happened. Of course, at the time the play was written Spain's parliament had been suspended for a number of years by the military dictator Primo de Rivera, whose rule (1923–1931) was the satirical target of this play. In the play, the lack of political activity and the imposition of censorship, presumably applied to events of real note, leads to the newspapers' sensationalist interest in anything remotely newsworthy. The atmosphere of drinking, gambling and theatre going also communicates this sense of a vacuum in public life. It is probably also a satirical reference to the habits of Primo de Rivera, as described by British historian Hugh Thomas: 'He would work enormously hard for weeks on end and then disappear for a *juerga* of dancing, drinking and love-making with gypsies. He would be observed almost alone in the streets of Madrid, swathed in an opera cloak, making his way from one café to another, and on returning home would issue a garrulous and sometimes even intoxicated communiqué – which he would often have to cancel in the morning' (2001, 26).

17 Another allusion to the crime of Captain Sánchez (see note 5 and Introduction p. 20).

18 'Revolante el velillo trotero' [a rough piece of flapping gauze]: 'Revolante' is not accepted by the DRAE, but seems to come from 'revolotear', to whirl around, and 'volar', to fly. 'Velillo' seems to be a diminutive of 'velo', meaning veil or thin

gauze, which is perhaps what the clothes are wrapped up in. 'Trotero' is only given as a noun in the DRAE, as an archaic word meaning a messenger or post boy. Here, as an adjective, it seems to derive from 'trote', where 'de mucho trote' means hard wearing or tough.

19 'Sombrerotes y zamarras' [peasants' garb]: a 'sombrerote' is a large wide-brimmed hat; a 'zamarra' is a rustic sheepskin jacket. Perhaps more important than the specific details of the items of clothing mentioned is the suggestion that the people in question (all involved in rural industries – cheese, honey, *etc*.) are of peasant stock.

20 A *duro* was worth five pesetas.

21 The pawnbrokers they visit is on the Calle de la Montera, between the Puerta del Sol and the Red de San Luis where it meets the Gran Vía. Since the early 20th century it has been notorious for prostitution. Even today it is lined with prostitutes and burly men offering to buy gold.

22 Gran Peña: Another iconic building of the early 20th century. It was built in 1917 to accommodate the private and exclusive Gran Peña club, opened in 1914. Both the Gran Peña and the Círculo de Bellas Artes are located on or very near to the Gran Vía, a wide boulevard built to connect the Calle de Alcalá with the Plaza de España. Though plans for the Gran Vía were drawn up in the mid-19th century, it was not completed until 1929.

23 '¡Tan incentiva pintura los sentidos me enajena!' [Who will not change a raven for a dove?]: This is a parody of Don Juan's words to Brígida in Zorrilla's *Don Juan Tenorio* (Act II, sc. ix): "Tan incentiva pintura / los sentidos me enajena, / y el alma ardiente me llena / de su insensata pasión." [Such an enticing picture disturbs my senses, and my ardent soul fills me with insane passion]. The idea Valle-Inclán seems to be conveying is, 'Who could resist such a honeytrap?' The words 'Who will not change a raven for a dove?' are spoken by Lysander to Helena in Shakespeare's *A Midsummer Night's Dream*. The words convey the sense that there is a much better option available, one that is so tempting as to be irresistible; and of course Lysander's 'sentidos' [senses] are literally 'enajenados' [disturbed] by the enchantment that has induced him to fall in love with Helena. The question also appropriately conveys the irony and cynicism of using words conceived in love in a situation defined by greed and self-interest.

24 'Un heroico Príncipe de la Milicia': an ironic analogy between the General and Saint Michael the Archangel. A prince of the Celestial Army, Saint Michael is often depicted as a warrior casting Lucifer and his rebellious angels out of hell or battling the heathen.

25 A *guajira* is a Cuban folk song about country life (such as the well-known 'Guantanamera').

26 Cardona and Zahareas note that the fictional *El Constitucional*, owned by Don Alfredo Toledano, is possibly a substitute for the real newspaper *El Liberal*, owned by Don Alfredo Vicenti (201). It may also be sending up a range of liberal newspapers including *El Imparcial* and *España Nueva*, which revealed and then pursued the gory details of Captain Sánchez's crime. A number of real Spanish newspapers are mentioned in the play, including 'la Corres' (*Correspondencia de España*), the *Heraldo* and *El Diario Universal*.

27 See the introduction for the significance of this allusion to the Cuban war (p. 24).

28 'Huyo veloz como la corza herida. / ¡Orégano sea!' [I make haste like a hart or a roe! / Over spice-scented hills may you go!]: Senabre observes that 'Huyo veloz como la corza herida' is a perfect hendecasyllable, and is probably a parodic quote from an unknown source. 'Orégano sea' comes from the saying, 'creer que todo el monte es orégano', which translates roughly as to think that life is a bowl of cherries, suggesting that he's wishing him luck. My translation parodies a line from the Song of Solomon 8:14: 'Make haste, my beloved, and be thou like to a roe or to a young hart upon the mountains of spices' (King James Bible), a verse which is also sent up in P. G. Wodehouse's *Jeeves and the Feudal Spirit* (103).

29 'Yo me najo para cambiar de vitola en el Aguila' [Next stop: swanky threads]: Almacenes El Aguila was a large department store opened in 1919 on Madrid's main shopping street, the Calle de Preciados, where the Corte Inglés can be found today.

30 Evidently the 'dodger' is a reference to the 'artful dodger' of Dickens' *Oliver Twist*. Valle-Inclán consistently juxtaposes respectable people and institutions with their low-life equivalents: so for example the Lout of the Green Baize is described by Valle as a 'chulapo', a word used to describe a lower-class native of Madrid in the 18th and 19th centuries. For this reason, the translation of 'camastrón' as 'Dodger' and 'quitolis' as 'Diver' (a pickpocket) is intended to get across the idea of a gang of thieves in the ironic context of a smart members' club devoted, at least in appearance, to the pursuit of culture.

31 Although, as we have seen, *Madrid Moderno* is the name of a specific part of the city associated with liberal and bourgeois values, I have allowed for the more general interpretation of 'Modern Madrid' in the translation given that the neighbourhood is used by Valle-Inclán as a synecdoche for Madrid, and perhaps even for Spain, itself.

32 The first Conde de Romanones (1863–1950) was a Spanish liberal who occupied a variety of high profile positions in government during his political career. He was President of the Senate when Primo de Rivera staged his coup in 1923. In 1903 he founded a politically partial newspaper named *El Diario Universal*, referred to here by Valle-Inclán. According to Francisco Umbral, Valle detested Romanones as 'el gran liberal,' but admired 'su picardía, su "mundo", su cinismo y su inteligencia y gracia' [his roguishness, his worldliness, his cynicism, his intelligence and wit] (69).

33 The Hospital de la Inclusa (also known as Nuestra Señora de la Inclusa) was a home for abandoned and orphaned babies located in the Puerta del Sol area of Madrid. The hilarious inappropriateness of the apprentice's new role as a wet nurse is perhaps a reference to the Conde de Romanones' tendency to find unusual roles for individuals under his protection (Varela Ortega 2001, 169).

34 'Un hotel en Vicálvaro' [a little house on the outskirts of town]: once a small town absorbed into the city during the 19th century, Vicálvaro became a district in the southeast of Madrid. It became headquarters to the cavalry of Spain's newly established police service or Guardia Civil in 1844. It also witnessed Leopoldo O'Donnell's 1854 coup named, precisely, *La Vicalvarada*, which led to Spain's

Bienio progresista (two years of government by the Progressives rather than the Moderates, favoured by Isabel II). This is therefore another example of Valle-Inclán's loading of his references to the urban geography of Madrid with historical allusions to the relatively recent past.

35   'Ésos ya quieren llevarse el suceso al distrito de Canillejas' [These people are trying to shift all the attention out to some remote suburb]: Canillejas is an affluent suburb to the east of Madrid whose population doubled during the first two decades of the 20th century, and doubled again in the following two decades. Valle-Inclán seems to equate the central and suburban areas of Madrid with melodramas (*folletines*) and homespun comedies (*comedias caseras*) respectively.

36   The tax collector is a 'Vigilante de consumos', *i.e.* he is specifically in charge of collecting a highly unpopular, contentious and politically sensitive tax on food. This tax, first introduced in 1845, was finally abolished in 1911. As in *Luces de Bohemia* and elsewhere, Valle draws on the events of a number of years and meaningfully condenses them, often in simple allusions such as this one, into the action of his plays.

37   It is not entirely clear to whom the General is referring here, though it is clearly a parody of Primo de Rivera, who in his Barcelona manifesto of 1923 declared his devotion to the interests of Spain: '[...] the time has come to give heed to the anxiety, to respond to the urgent demands of all those who, loving the mother country, see for her no other salvation than deliverance from the professional politicians [...] we shall now assume entire responsibility and the nation shall be governed by us or by civilians who represent our morality and our principles. Enough, now, of gentle rebellions which, without remedying anything, damage as much or more than that strong and virile discipline to which we ardently devote ourselves for Spain and for the King.' (Cowans 2003, 126–27)

38   '¡Un viva la Virgen, señora, va a salvar el Trono de San Fernando!' [This *bon viveur*, madam, will save the Throne of Saint Ferdinand!]. Cardona and Zahareas explain that the absent 'señora' to whom the General addresses his comments is probably Victoria of Battenberg, wife of King Alfonso XIII, who did not support the suspension of parliamentary democracy under Primo de Rivera (1970, 209). Within the context of the play, however, perhaps the General is already imagining the constituency of supporters later represented by Doña Simplicia. Saint Ferdinand is patron saint of the Military and the Monarchy in Spain.

39   The 'Húsares de Pavía' regiment was created in 1684 to serve in Spain's Italian colonies and was named after the Spanish victory over the French army at Pavia, Italy.

40   'Un pronunciamiento isabelino' [the kind of coup we've had in the past]: There was a series of military coups under Isabel II (reigned 1833–1868), largely owing to the fact that she abused her position to ensure that only her favoured party of Moderates could get the necessary majority to take the reins of power. Army Generals in this context became the 'espadas' or 'swords' of political factions. After the Restoration of the monarchy in 1874 under Isabel's son, Alfonso XII, the electoral system was rigged to allow for a peaceful alternation of power between the Liberal and Conservative parties and so prevent the army from interfering in

politics. However, by the end of the Restoration period the army had once again begun to have a decisive influence in the political arena: in 1917, with the creation of the trade-union inspired *Juntas de Defensa*, and again in 1923, with Primo de Rivera's military coup. General Franco's rebellion against the Second Republic in 1936 was therefore the last in a long line of military interventions since the 19th century.

41   The name 'Camarasa' is, as we would expect, comical in this context: the quick-fire sequence of syllables ending in -*a* lends it a barking, military sound. 'Cama rasa' also means 'low bed', alluding presumably to the Colonel's low physical stature. Finally, a 'soldado raso' is equivalent to a private, so undermining his military rank.

42   'Demasiada goma' [An orgy of silks and satins]: According to Senabre, 'goma' derives from 'gomoso', meaning an effeminate dandy. Here he indicates that it is used collectively to indicate 'gente elegante, bien ataviada' [elegant, well-dressed people]. (1990, 296)

43   Isabel de Borbón y Borbón, princess of Asturias and Isabel II's eldest daughter, was affectionately known as 'la chata' due to her snub nose.

44   'Spanish heroines': Doña Simplicia lists Teresa de Jesús (also known as Teresa de Ávila or Santa Teresa, the mystical poet); María Pita (who fought the English at La Coruña in 1589); Agustina de Aragón (who fought to defend a besieged Zaragoza during the War of Independence); and Mariana Pineda (executed in 1831 for embroidering on a flag the liberal slogan 'Ley, Libertad, Igualdad' [Law, Liberty, Equality].

45   As Dian Fox tells us, many of the Golden Age playwright Calderón's plays 'resolutely defy the principle of the divine right of kings' (1986, 117).

46   Valle's description of the King is designed to make him sound like a peasant: his smile is 'belfona' (a 'belfo' is a horse's muzzle); his eyes are 'pardillos', suggesting naivety but also 'pardo', the colour of earth; when he applauds he is 'campechano', meaning genial but evoking 'campesinos' or peasants; his body is 'alombrigada' or worm-like; and his voice is like a hollow reed. The 'carátula' (mask) of his face and the quality of his voice are highly reminiscent of Tirano Banderas, the eponymous tyrant of Valle-Inclán's most famous novel, written at more or less the same time as this play (1926).

47   The name of the 'local rag' is *El Lábaro de Orbaneja*, suggesting its allegiance to Primo de Rivera, whose maternal surname was Orbaneja (Senabre 1990, 298).

Printed and bound by CPI Group (UK) Ltd, Croydon, CR0 4YY

13/04/2025